"You should have won an Oscar,"

Brett snapped. "Your performance on the boat coming over here was magnificent!"

Loris was shocked. *He* was the one who had put on an act—leading her to believe he loved her, wooing her on the moonlit deck. She longed to talk to him, but she didn't want to let him see how hurt she was. She had been so naive—well, not anymore!

"I've told you before that I don't want you to talk to me," she said. "It's none of your business what I do with my life."

"At one time you led me to believe it was. But then I'm forgetting what a marvelous actress you are. I wonder," he said with a touch of malice, "if you can repeat the performance?"

Before she knew what he meant to do, he pulled her close and crushed her mouth beneath his....

Other titles by

RACHEL LINDSAY
IN HARLEQUIN PRESENTS

Other titles by

RACHEL LINDSAY
IN HARLEQUIN ROMANCES

RACHEL LINDSAY

the widening stream

Harlequin Books

TORONTO•LONDON•NEW YORK•AMSTERDAM
SYDNEY•HAMBURG•PARIS•STOCKHOLM

Harlequin Presents edition published March 1980
ISBN 0-373-10346-8

Original hardcover edition published in 1952
by Hutchinson & Co. Ltd.

CHAPTER I

Loris Cameron leant against the rails of the ship and looked out across the gradually widening expanse of grey water at the coastline of England receding farther and farther into the distance. The hooting of the ship's siren seemed to echo mournfully in her heart as for the first time in her twenty-three years she watched the shores of home fade, and her grey eyes held a hint of sadness as she gazed at them. Then with a faint sigh she turned away and stepped through the hatchway leading down to her cabin.

As she entered her stateroom the girl who was gazing out of the porthole window turned excitedly towards her.

"Isn't it thrilling, Loris? I can hardly believe we're off at last."

"If you'd been up on deck with me you'd have been even more thrilled. It's incredible a ship of this size could get through such a narrow dock."

"I'm thrilled enough already without bothering about the silly ship. Just imagine, in four days from now we shall be in New York and I'll see Dickson!"

She pirouetted gleefully round the room, strewing flimsy pieces of lingerie haphazardly on the floor behind her.

Loris bent and retrieved them, putting them methodically on the bed. "Go and lie down, dear. I'll unpack for you." She gave the small figure a gentle push. "Go along, Melanie, lie down."

With a little grimace of protest Melanie obediently settled herself on the bed nearest the porthole, slim legs curled beneath her as she watched Loris unpack.

The two made a striking contrast to each other, the one tall and dark, the other small and fair. One might have wondered how girls so totally unlike each other in every way should have come to be travelling companions at all, for the younger, with her startling fair hair and chocolate-box prettiness, was totally different from the dark, quiet girl several years her senior.

"I don't know how I'd manage without you, Loris."

Loris laughed. "Your mother could easily have found someone else to keep an eye on you."

"I dare say, but no one I'd have liked being with half as much as you, I can't think of you as a chaperone at all."

"I should hope not! If I'd thought coming on this trip would make you think of me as some sort of ogre, I wouldn't have accepted the offer."

Melanie jumped up and hugged her impulsively. "Of course you're not an ogre, silly! I'm delighted Mummy wouldn't let me travel on my own. Think how much more fun I shall have now I've got you to share it with."

"Hey, hey, you don't have to strangle me!" Loris disengaged herself laughingly, then went on in a tone of mock severity: "But you must do what I tell you, or it's bread and water for you, my child!"

With a gurgle of amusement Melanie settled herself back on the bed. "You know, Loris," she said, suddenly serious, "I was awfully surprised the vicar let you come at all."

"So was I," Loris replied pensively.

Her thoughts went back to her kindly, gentle father, alone now in his rambling old vicarage; back to that April morning nearly a month ago when she had been working in the garden and Melanie's mother had telephoned to ask her to go over and see her. She had hastily brushed the earth from her old skirt and set off on her bicycle to the imposing red-brick house where the Powells lived.

Loris had been a thin, motherless child of nine when the Powells had moved to the village of Roxborough fourteen years before. It was from her father's housekeeper that she had first heard about the Powells' little daughter, and being a solitary child had eagerly awaited an invitation to visit these wealthy and imposing strangers, imagining Melanie a little girl like herself, hungry for companionship.

She remembered her first meeting with Melanie and how disappointed she had been at the sight of the little four-year-old who had come into the room with her nurse. Here was no companion for walks in the wood, no friend with whom to share her joys and secrets. But Mrs. Powell had an acute knowledge of children and with her mother's instinct immediately sensed the older child's disappointment.

Gently she pushed the two children together and her little daughter threw chubby arms around the other girl's neck. From that moment Loris had been Melanie's slave and the two became inseparable, their friendship surviving the separation when Melanie was sent away to an expensive boarding-school and Loris remained at Roxborough to attend the day-school three miles away.

When she left school Loris stayed at home to help her father with his parochial duties.

It was a busy but uneventful life, and she was thankful when Melanie came home from finishing school to lend a note of gaiety to the village with her many friends and gay parties.

It was at one of these parties that she met and fell in love with Dickson Loftus, a lanky American boy of twenty-four. But though her parents were delighted with the match, for Mrs. Powell had known Dickson's mother when they were single, they only agreed to their daughter's engagement on condition that she did not marry till she was twenty-one, and remained adamant in spite of Melanie's pleading. Melanie grew so pale and thin at the separation that her parents decided to take her to California in the spring prior to her twenty-first birthday, and it was a great blow to them all when Mr. Powell suddenly succumbed to a heart attack and was forbidden to travel.

7

Faced on the one hand with the job of nursing an invalid husband back to health, and on the other with a tearful daughter, Mrs. Powell decided to let Melanie go to California and stay with her future parents-in-law until she and her husband could follow her out for the wedding. But they were unwilling to let her travel alone, and her mother looked around for someone to go with her. Her first choice was Loris, and she was greatly surprised when the girl politely but firmly declined.

"It's very kind of you to ask me, Mrs. Powell, but I'm afraid my father couldn't do without me."

"But, my dear, do you really think your father would want you to sacrifice. . . ."

"Oh, it's not a question of sacrifice or anything as heroic as that," Loris interrupted. "It's just that I wouldn't feel happy leaving him alone. He's so helpless in the house – I don't even think he knows how to boil an egg!" And in spite of everything Mrs. Powell could find to say, Loris was firm in her refusal, and cycled back to the vicarage resolutely refusing to think of the wonderful chance she had just turned down.

Her father came into the shabby lounge just as she was pouring out the tea, and she did not notice the searching look he gave her.

"Did you see Melanie today?" he asked casually, settling himself in an armchair.

"No. She went up to town."

"Oh. Any other news?"

"No, Daddy, nothing important. I saw old Sam Sykes in the High Street this afternoon and he said his rheumatism is so much better he'll be coming along to choir practice tonight."

"I see." There was a pause, then: "Why didn't you tell me you'd refused Mrs. Powell's offer to go to America?"

Loris put her cup down with a little clatter and moved across to the window. "I didn't think Mrs. Powell would tell you."

"There was no need to keep it secret, my dear," her father said reprovingly. "Surely it was the most natural thing in the world for you to tell me?"

Loris gave what she hoped was an indifferent shrug. "I didn't even want to bother you with such a silly idea. It's quite impossible. I've too much to do to become nursemaid to Melanie, darling though she is."

With a little sigh the Reverend Francis Cameron stood up and moving over to his daughter put out a gentle hand and turned her face to his. "Look at me, child. I've tried to care for you as well as I could since your mother died and I've always prided myself on having done a pretty good job. It wasn't until Mrs. Powell told me you'd refused her offer that I began to feel that I must have failed you in some way."

"But, Daddy...."

"Let me finish, Loris. Travelling is something nearly every girl longs for, and no normal person would refuse an opportunity if it came their way. The fact that you did seems to tell me I must have failed you."

"But, Daddy, that's absurd! I'd love to go to America. I only refused because I thought you wouldn't be able to get along without me."

If her father privately agreed with her, he did not say so. A widower for twenty years, no one meant more to him than Loris and he had watched her grow up from a solemn-faced child into a sensitive young woman, filled with pride at her intelligence. But it was borne upon him now that she was as much a stranger to him in some ways as any other young woman. An ascetic man, he had not realized that his way of life, satisfying as it was to him, was not suitable for his daughter, and only now did he realize how much gaiety and youthful companionship she had been missing. When Mrs. Powell had spoken to him over the telephone after Loris's visit he had seen her as an adult individual for the first time, realizing not only how much she had already missed for his sake but how much more she was prepared to miss in the future unless he prevented it.

He smiled reprovingly and shook his head. "What a conceited young person you are, my darling, to think I couldn't manage without you! I'm not so helpless that I won't be able to look after myself while you're away."

"But, Daddy, you know very well you've already got as much as you can do with the parish."

"If it comes to that, Mrs. Parkin can come in and look after me. Her husband died three months ago and she's looking for a job and somewhere to live – I'm sure she'll only be too glad to come as my housekeeper. It would be good for Melanie if you went with her, Loris – she's highly strung and she needs a steadying influence behind her."

"Heavens, Daddy, you make me feel so staid and old-fashioned!"

"You are, my dear." He gave her an affectionate pat. "That's another reason why you should go. It'd be good for *you*, too. You ought to enjoy yourself with other young people. Mrs. Powell wants you to stay in California until she and her husband can go out themselves and I expect you'll have a great deal of fun. Now run along and ring her up and tell her you've changed your mind."

Loris threw her arms around him. "Oh, darling, you're the nicest father any girl could have – and I love you."

She ran out of the room and a moment later he heard her voice, eager and excited on the telephone. With a sigh, Francis Cameron went into his study and closed the door behind him. His daughter's absence would leave an aching void in his life which only her return would fill, but he was determined not to let her know this, and in the weeks of preparation which followed hid his feelings so well that no one guessed at the sadness he felt.

At the memory of how fervently her father had kissed her good-bye, Loris jerked her thoughts back to the present and continued unpacking for Melanie.

The girls had exclaimed with pleasure when they had first seen their walnut-panelled stateroom with its narrow twin beds, perfectly appointed bathroom with taps for hot, cold and sea-water; and now that the cabin was littered with Melanie's clothes it seemed to have lost its impersonal atmosphere. By the time Loris had finished unpacking they were well out to sea, and looking through the porthole, she caught a glimpse of the expanse of heaving water. The ship had fallen into its steady rhythm and the pulsation of the engines was settling into an even throb.

She glanced down at her watch. "Heavens, it's half past one! If we don't hurry we won't get any lunch."

Hastily they made their way down the companionway to the restaurant and were filled with awe at the size of the beautifully decorated room, Loris in particular finding it a delight to sit down to a meal she had not had to prepare with her own hands.

Later they went up to the top deck and spent the rest of the afternoon watching their fellow passengers, and it was nearly six o'clock before they returned to their cabin.

"Hallo, what's this?" Melanie bent and picked up an envelope which had been slipped under the door during their absence. "Somebody's writing to me already!" she said, with naïve conceit.

"Probably from the Purser asking you to collect something," Loris replied drily.

Melanie tore open the envelope and took out a single sheet of paper. Then she looked up with an excited laugh. "You'll never guess who it's from, Loris! It's a friend of Dickson's. Here, read it."

Loris took the note and read the firm handwriting.

Dear Miss Powell, it began.

Glancing through the passenger list I noticed your name and wonder if you are the same Melanie Powell who is engaged to a friend of mine by the name of Dickson Loftus. I saw Dickson just before I came over to

11

England and he told me he was expecting his fiancée quite soon. As yours is such an uncommon name I'm hoping you are the same girl and am taking the liberty of writing to ask you if you will have a drink with me in the Observation Lounge before dinner tonight. I shall be at a table by the window and will have a copy of the passenger list before me to help you to recognize me. I look forward to the pleasure of meeting you, but if I am mistaken in thinking you are Dickson's fiancée, a note to Cabin A.27 will suffice.

Yours –

Brett Halliday.

Loris handed the note back. "What are you going to do?"

"Do? Why, go and meet him, of course! Think of all the things he'll have to tell me."

"But you don't even know him."

Melanie burst out laughing. "Oh, Loris, how cautious you are! We can't possibly come to any harm just by going to meet him. After all, he doesn't know us by sight, so we can walk through the lounge and if we don't like the look of him we needn't stop at his table."

"You think of everything, Melanie! For one so young, you're an adept in guile."

That evening Loris was nervous and hesitant as they entered the crowded Observation Lounge, but Melanie seemed quite unconcerned, and ignored the interested eyes which followed them as they made their way across the room. Suddenly she gripped Loris's hand. "There he is!"

Looking in the direction of Melanie's pointing finger Loris found herself gazing into a pair of piercing eyes and suddenly, for no reason she could think of, her heart started to pound. "Are you sure that's the right man?" she whispered.

"Positive! He's got a copy of the passenger list in front of him. Doesn't look like a crook, does he?" Melanie whispered back. "Come on, let's go and introduce ourselves."

As if she had a sudden premonition of all that would befall her if she were to meet this man, Loris gave a shiver of apprehension.

"Oh, come on," Melanie said impatiently. "What's the matter now?"

"Perhaps a goose walked over my grave," Loris laughed shakily. "Don't mind me, it's probably first-night nerves. Let's go and meet him."

They advanced towards the table and the man stood up.

"Mr. Halliday?" Melanie asked.

"Yes. Are you Miss Powell?"

"That's right. And this is my friend, Miss Cameron."

They all smiled at each other and immediately felt more at ease. Brett Halliday drew up two chairs and within a few minutes Melanie was in earnest conversation with him, asking question after question about her fiancé – whether Dickson was well, how he liked being back in America after his European trip – all the hundred and one details a girl wants to know about the boy she loves.

Loris sat back and watched the man as he answered the spate of questions. She liked the clear, incisive way he spoke, surprised that the accent of his deep voice was quite English. Indeed, had it not been for a slight drawl, she would not have taken him for an American at all, and her curiosity must have shown in her face, for he suddenly turned to her.

"Is anything worrying you, Miss Cameron?"

She gave a guilty start. "Not at all, Mr. Halliday. Why do you ask?"

"I just wondered why you were gazing at me so earnestly," he grinned. "I hope you don't take me for a confidence trickster?"

Loris blushed painfully. "I beg your pardon, I didn't realize I was staring. It was only that your English accent

13

puzzled me."

"That's easily explained, Miss Cameron. My mother was English and I was educated in England."

She flushed again, stung by the slight mockery in his tone. But Melanie appeared not to notice it and rushed into the silence with more questions about Dickson, leaving Loris to study Halliday covertly as he turned away.

Apart from occasional visits to relatives in London and Scotland, Loris had spent all her life at the vicarage, and her experience of the world was very limited. She had met few men, and certainly none had ever impressed her as deeply as this complete stranger.

She judged him to be about thirty-five. His wavy dark hair sprang back from a high forehead and his mouth was mobile and firm. Erect, she had taken him to be about six feet tall and had noticed his athletic build and easy stance, The hands playing with the stem of his glass were thin and brown and his movements were confident and casual. Suddenly she felt his eyes upon her again – those piercing hazel eyes which seemed to look right through her.

"Do you find me so out of the ordinary, Miss Cameron?" he demanded quizzically.

Melanie burst out laughing. "Oh, you mustn't mind Loris, Mr. Halliday! She's spent all her life in a country vicarage and I'm afraid she's terribly unworldly. If she's staring at you it's probably because she's trying to fit you into a little pigeon-hole. She feels safer if she can label people."

"Loris," Brett Halliday murmured. "What an unusual name."

"Yes, isn't it?" Melanie said effusively. "I can't imagine her called anything else, though. I don't think it's too bad, do you?"

"On the contrary, I think it's one of the loveliest names I've ever heard." He turned to Loris. "You must forgive me if I seem rude, but I've never come across it before."

For a long moment the man and the girl looked at

14

one another, grey eyes staring into hazel. Loris felt as if his gaze penetrated the surface of her mind, revealing her very thoughts and drawing them out, and it was with an effort that she dropped her eyes, feeling as she did so that in that moment two spirits had touched.

The rest of the evening was hazy to her, although she vaguely remembered going into dinner with Melanie and meeting Brett Halliday afterwards for coffee in the lounge. She sat listening to her friend's excited chatter and the man's amused replies, but seldom joined in the conversation, and it was nearly eleven o'clock when she decided they had better go to bed; for the strangeness and excitement of the day had tired them both, and she did not like the hectic flush colouring Melanie's thin cheeks.

"Come along, darling, it's time we went." Loris stood up and held out her hand to the man and her fingers were imprisoned in his warm grasp. "Good night, Mr. Halliday. It's been so nice meeting you."

Still holding Loris's hand, Brett Halliday turned to Melanie. "I can't let you go off like this without arranging to see you both again. How about meeting me on the Sun Deck in the morning? Have you booked your deck chairs yet? You haven't? Well, we'd better see about it first thing tomorrow. I'll be on deck about ten-thirty and I'll look out for you."

As they made their way out of the lounge his eyes followed the tall, slim figure of the dark-haired girl. "Loris Cameron," he murmured to himself. "Loris. What a lovely name."

When they had disappeared he took out a cigarette, and tapping it reflectively on the back of his hand before he lit it, settled back in an armchair and picked up a magazine. But a pair of wide-set grey eyes in a heart-shaped face remained in his mind long after he had forgotten all about Dickson's fiancée.

Loris meanwhile lay awake in her narrow bed, listening to the creaking of the timbers as the ship rolled gently

15

in the lap of the restless waves. Once again she seemed to feel those hazel eyes piercing through her, as though they saw into her very heart, and it was some time before she fell asleep, rocked into slumber by the tossing Atlantic.

CHAPTER II

LORIS was awakened next morning by the sun shining on to her eyelids through the porthole window and reaching out for her watch saw with surprise that it was nine o'clock. Unless they got up immediately they would be too late for breakfast. She debated whether to awaken Melanie or not and finally decided the poor child still looked so tired that it would be better to let her sleep on. She dressed quickly and quietly, but just as she was creeping out of the room Melanie awakened.

"Oh, Loris, I do feel peculiar! I've got the most dreadful headache and I think I'm going to be sick."

Loris went to her bedside and looked anxiously into the small, white face. "Perhaps you'd feel better if you had some tea and toast," she suggested gently.

But at the mention of food Melanie groaned. "For heaven's sake don't talk about breakfast! If you do, I'll make a complete fool of myself."

Her tone was so long-suffering that Loris laughed and Melanie herself gave a feeble grin. "I feel such an idiot, Loris, but I'm afraid I'm going to be terribly seasick."

"Don't let it worry you – you can't help being a bad sailor, it's just one of those things. I'll ring and have my breakfast sent down. Are you sure you won't have anything?"

"Positive."

Loris put her finger on the bell and when the stewardess came in she cast a professional eye upon the recumbent figure in bed. "There's nothing much the matter with your friend, miss," she told Loris. "I'll get something for her – just the thing for sea-sickness."

Melanie moved her head impatiently on the pillow. "Don't bother about having your breakfast sent down, Loris. I'd really much rather be alone. Anyway, we promised to meet Mr. Halliday on the Sun Deck at half past ten and he'll think it odd if neither of us appears."

Loris regarded her doubtfully. "Are you sure you'll be all right on your own? After all, your mother didn't ask me to come with you so I could gallivant while you're lying in bed."

"Oh, Loris, for heaven's sake! Mummy would want you to enjoy the trip as much as I do. It isn't as if I'm really ill. Hundreds of people get seasick."

"That's right," the stewardess interposed cheerfully. "One crossing last November only two people appeared in the dining-room the whole time. You go on up, miss. I'll keep an eye on the young lady for you."

"All right, then. I'll just have breakfast and find Mr. Halliday to make our apologies to him."

When Loris made her way up to the Sun Deck the sun was shining in a clear, blue sky. The ship scarcely seemed to be moving, but as she stepped out from under cover she was nearly knocked over by the force of the wind which beat against her. She dug her hands deeply into the pockets of her coat and buried her chin in the folds of her scarf as the wind flattened her skirts against her legs, whipping her hair into tiny tendrils that beat crazily against her face. As she battled her way along the deserted deck it seemed as though she were the only passenger to be struggling against the elements that morning. Making slow progress towards the bows, a particularly strong gust of wind nearly blew her off her feet, and with a feeling of complete helplessness she felt herself being driven towards the side.

"What a fool I'll look if I fall down!" she thought, and in that instant a pair of strong arms reached out and steadied her.

"Easy does it! I don't mind if women fall for me metaphorically, but it's liable to be embarrassing if they do it too literally."

As he spoke, the man pulled her against him shielding her from the force of the wind, and Loris found herself

18

gazing into Brett Halliday's eyes. With what dignity she could muster she drew away, only to be flattened against him by another gust of wind. Her head was buried against the rough tweed of his coat and she felt his breath warm against her cheek.

"Sorry," she said shakily. "Evidently I haven't found my sea-legs yet."

"Think nothing of it," he replied easily, drawing her into a more sheltered part of the deck. Before Loris knew what was happening he had dragged two deck chairs together and settled her into one of them, tucking a rug around her.

He sat down beside her and flipped open his cigarette case.

"Have one? Or don't you like American cigarettes?"

"No, thanks, I don't smoke at all."

"Ah." There was a note of satisfaction in his voice. "I rather thought you didn't. Where's your friend this morning?"

With a start Loris realized she had completely forgotten about Melanie. "And here I am," she thought, "allowing myself to be settled next to him as though he had expressly invited *me*."

"Melanie isn't feeling very well," she explained hastily. "She's staying in bed, so I just came up to tell you and make our apologies." She made a movement to free herself from the rug, but a firm arm came across the chair and prevented her.

"You don't have to get in such a frenzy about it, honey. I guess there's no need for you to run away so soon, is there? You act as if I'm going to eat you!"

With his voice low and amused, his drawl was even more pronounced. "Insufferable man!" thought Loris, and looked down helplessly at the tweed-clad arm resting so firmly across her chair.

"I must go down to Melanie. I really can't leave her alone any longer," she said with determination.

"But I'm sure she wouldn't want to keep you in the

cabin the whole time, would she?"

"Oh no. She insisted on my coming. . . ." Loris stopped abruptly.

"You see?" There was gentle irony in his tone. "You're not a good liar, Miss Cameron. Do you dislike me so much that you can't bear the idea of my company for a morning?"

"Oh no, it isn't that at all. It's just that. . . ."

"Just what? Go on." And then, as she did not speak, he bent closer. "Or are you afraid I might believe you *wanted* to stay with me?" She still did not answer, and he went on: "Be honest, honey. You wanted to see me again almost as much as I wanted to see you. Isn't that so?"

Lifting her eyes, she saw an urgent sincerity in his face which belied the flippancy of his tone.

"You still haven't answered me, Loris."

But her voice when she did answer was so low that he had to bend forward to hear it.

"I – I didn't think there was any need for me to answer it."

For a moment their eyes held. Then Brett moved his arm away from her chair and settled himself back into his own.

"Well, honey, now that I'm not afraid you're going to run away we can take things more easily!"

As if glad of release from the tension they both laughed.

"I won't run away, Mr. –"

"The name's Brett," he said quickly. "You'll have to get used to calling me that, so you may as well start now. I do believe you're still shy!"

Loris flushed. "I'm not really. It's just that things have happened so quickly I don't know where I am."

"I'm sorry if I've rushed you, honey, but I'm not a very patient man and I had the feeling that unless I used shock tactics you'd run away so fast I'd never be able to catch you." His face lit up with a brilliant smile. "You aren't the sort of girl I'd want to rush, but I was sure about you the first moment we met, and I had a feeling it was the same way with you."

Subterfuge seemed unnecessary. It was as if they both knew they had waited all their lives for this meeting, and Loris gave him a slow smile which transfigured her face.

While Melanie was still confined to the cabin Brett and Loris spent every moment together. As the ship ploughed its way across the Atlantic they dined and danced, went for walks on the Sun Deck, or when the Gulf Stream brought warmth and humidity, lazed on deck chairs, talking idly or lying in companionable silence. For Loris it was a time of enchantment. The realization that she was a woman with a woman's ability to inspire love in a man's heart gave her a sense of confidence she had never felt before. In those few days Loris grew up and left behind for ever the safe, sheltered garden of her girlhood to embark on the more hazardous course of a woman.

Sensitive to her shyness and inexperience, Brett did not attempt to make love to her at first. It was as if he sensed that by revealing the passion of which he was capable he would make her withdraw into herself and he accepted the tender little advances she made towards him without allowing himself to lose the gentle solicitude which hid his desire.

On the last night of the voyage Melanie tried to get up, but the motion of the boat soon sent her back to bed.

"It looks as if I'll have to stay here until we dock," she said ruefully.

Loris stroked her hair affectionately. "It's a shame, darling. You haven't been able to enjoy the trip at all."

"In a way I have." Melanie's eyes twinkled. "I've enjoyed watching you!"

"Watching me?"

"Yes. Don't you think I saw from the very first moment you met Brett Halliday you fell in love with him?

21

You see, you're blushing!" She laughed gleefully. "It's a good thing I've been laid up, so you two could be on your own!"

Loris joined in her laughter and hugged her, but Melanie pulled herself eagerly away. "Has he told you he loves you?" she asked. "Has he proposed to you yet? Oh, Loris, I've been dying to ask you, but didn't dare!"

Loris walked over to the dressing-table and ran a comb through her hair, refusing to meet the girl's glance. She had wondered when Brett would let down his barrier of reserve, hoping he might say something about the future before the voyage was over and secretly afraid that as far as he was concerned it was merely a shipboard romance, a love affair which would peter out when they went ashore. Melanie's eager questions, bringing into the open what she had striven to hide even from herself, made her realize how frail were the threads which bound Brett to her, and with a throb of fear she recalled that he had never even taken her into his arms and kissed her.

Straightening the folds of her dress, she moved away from the mirror. "Don't be a nosy-parker," she said in mock reproof, and tweaked a lock of the fair hair. "Are you getting up for supper?"

"I don't think so." Melanie snuggled down. "I may as well spend the last few hours here. After all, you must have the last evening alone with Brett."

Loris left the cabin a few minutes later, her spirits soaring as she went to meet Brett. They dined, that last night, in the Veranda Grill, the windows open to the dark sky and cool breeze, and later walked along the Sun Deck to the part they had made their own particular retreat.

Lovingly Loris regarded Brett's finely etched profile as they stood idly at the rail together, the tip of his cigarette glowing in a vivid point of light as it travelled up to his lips. She looked out over the dark water shimmering under the moon and the breeze lifted her hair from her shoulders, letting it fall softly back again and rustling the skirt of her white dress.

With a sudden movement Brett threw away his cigarette and drew her into his arms. Loris leant against him, his nearness overwhelming her, feeling the hard maleness of his skin as he pressed his cheek against hers.

"I've wanted to do this for such a long time, my darling. But you're such a shy little thing that I was afraid of frightening you. Do you remember how scared you were that first morning on the Sun Deck? You didn't know whether to run away from me or humour me like an idiot child!"

"I never thought of you as an idiot or a child, Brett. It was just that your suddenness surprised me."

"I suppose it *was* rather surprising. But when you know me better you'll realize that once I make up my mind about anything I never sit back and wait for it to drop into my lap. You aren't smart or sophisticated, Loris, but the moment I saw you I knew neither of us could fight against what was going to happen. Our falling in love was as inevitable as night following day, and no one can stop the moon rising."

Dawning wonder shone in Loris's eyes. "It seems unbelievable that you should fall in love with me. You must have met so many other girls who can give you much more than I can."

"I have met them, Loris, and sometimes I thought I'd found what I was looking for. But none of them had your honesty and sweetness, none of them loved me for what I was, only for what I could give them. You've never asked me about my past or my future, you've taken me on trust for what I am."

"Your past belongs to you, Brett."

"And my future belongs to you, my heart."

Brett's words let loose an uprising of emotion she could not stem. He had opened the floodgates to all the love her young heart was longing to give and she did not attempt to hide the adoration in her eyes.

23

His arms tightened around her. "You are real, aren't you, Loris?"

"Quite real, Brett. Why don't you find out?"

"Aren't you shy any longer?" he asked tenderly.

"A little. You see, no one's ever made love to me before."

"And I'll make sure no one else ever does! You're mine, Loris, mine," he murmured urgently. "I'm the only one who's going to teach you how to love."

With an incoherent exclamation his mouth came down hungrily on hers. A swift shudder ran through her body and her lips trembled and then, after an instant, responded to his as her arms encircled his neck and she gave herself tremulously up to his embrace. His kiss deepened, thrilling her to an ecstasy she had never dreamt of, and she moved closer into the circle of his arms.

With a sudden convulsive movement Brett put her away from him. "Here endeth the first lesson," he said thickly.

With a little murmur Loris buried her face against his shoulder. "Oh, Brett, I love you," she breathed.

"And I love you, my darling. Which is why I'm going to send you to bed right now. I want to go on kissing you, but I'm afraid of myself."

She looked up at him with startled eyes. "But I want to stay with you."

"I know. And I want you to."

"Then why. . .?"

"When we're both old and grey I'll tell you why." He smiled and tilted her chin up gently. "Come along, darling, I'll see you to your cabin."

Loris gave a last look at the pale moon shedding its ghostly light on the deserted deck and knew that as long as she lived she would never forget the beauty of that moment. Then Brett took her arm and they walked slowly towards the companionway.

In the hustle and bustle of departure next morning Loris could not get away to find Brett, for Melanie was so excited at the prospect of seeing Dickson that she was of little help, and Loris found herself battling alone with passports, tickets and Customs officials. She caught a glimpse of Brett once in the distance, but although he tried to make his way towards her he was lost in the crowd of passengers who were disembarking. When their luggage was ready and checked the two girls stood together on the quayside, but although Melanie darted forward at the sight of any tall, fair young man, Dickson did not appear. It was only when they had almost given up hope of being met that an elderly couple came towards them.

Melanie ran to greet them and a few moments later returned excitedly to Loris. "It's Dickson's father and mother, Loris! I recognized them from their photographs. They say Dickson can't meet me, so they've come instead. Isn't it kind of them to fly all the way from California?"

Mr. and Mrs. Loftus came up and introduced themselves and Loris was relieved to find they were a friendly and cordial couple. The woman was plump and handsome, her grey hair elegantly dressed, but it seemed to Loris that she smiled with an effort and there was the same look of strain on her husband's face.

With Mr. Loftus to help them with their luggage they were soon speeding in a cab through down-town New York, and Melanie looked excitedly out of the window.

"Look, Loris, there's Sak's, and Bergdorf Goodman! Isn't it wonderful to see places you've heard about for so long?"

But Loris was hardly able to take in the brief glimpses of the great stores and skyscrapers which flashed by, and several times looked covertly at Mr. and Mrs. Loftus, who were sitting silently in the back of the cab. For some reason she could not fathom a nameless foreboding began to tug at her and she was thankful that in the excitement of their arrival Melanie had not questioned them too closely about their son.

Suddenly Melanie turned to Mrs. Loftus. "Mummy said we'd be staying in New York at the Plaza for a few days. I didn't know it was so far from the harbour. Isn't the driver taking us the wrong way?"

Mrs. Loftus seemed to hesitate. "Well, my dear, as Dickson couldn't come and meet you, my husband and I thought it would be a pity if you were to stay in New York just now. We knew you'd rather come here with Dickson later on, so my husband got us reservations on the afternoon plane for Los Angeles."

"You mean we're flying straight out to California?" In an exuberance of high spirits Melanie gave the woman a resounding kiss. "Oh, I'm so glad, Mrs. Loftus! I'm dying to see Dickson. Not that it wasn't sweet of you to meet us instead," she added hastily, "but I was so looking forward. . . ."

"I expect Dickson's been detained on business," Loris interrupted, seeing the girl's lips tremble. "I'm sure you won't mind waiting another few hours before you see him, will you?"

Grateful for Loris's tact, Mrs. Loftus gave her a brief smile. "That's right, Melanie – Dickson was detained. He's waiting for us in California."

Satisfied with this, Melanie looked out of the window again, and Loris regarded Mrs. Loftus in silent inquiry. The older woman gave her a little nod and whispered: "I'll speak to you when we get out of the cab."

That something was wrong was obvious – something to do with Dickson – and Loris felt her nameless fears crystallizing. It seemed to her as if the journey would never end, but at last the cab reached the airport, and drew up at the entrance to the section marked 'Pan-America'. They got out, thankful to ease their cramped legs, and Melanie, clinging to Mr. Loftus's arm, went off with him to see about their departure.

It was then that Mrs. Loftus turned to Loris, her face drawn and agitated. "I can't tell you how grateful I am for helping me to answer the child. I'd never have had the courage to tell her."

"Tell her what?" Loris asked apprehensively.

"That Dickson couldn't meet you because he's...."
She broke off and half turned away to regain control of
herself, then went on more steadily: "Dickson was involved in a car accident ten days ago. We didn't wire
the Powells because it didn't seem serious enough for
you to change your plans. He rested up for a few days
and was supposed to get up for the first time the day you
were due to sail. We had lunch as usual that day and I
couldn't understand why Dickson didn't come down, because he never liked to lie in bed unless he had to, so I
went upstairs to see if anything was the matter." She
pressed a handkerchief to her lips and Loris saw that her
hands were trembling. "I found him lying on the floor.
At first I thought he'd fainted or fallen over. But he was
all right – he was quite all right. He'd simply lost the
use of his legs."

"Lost the use of his legs?" Loris echoed.

"Yes. We've called in the finest specialists in the country and they all say the same thing. There's nothing
wrong with Dickson, nothing physically wrong at all.
He just can't walk, and they don't know why!"

At the pent-up misery in the woman's face Loris put
her arm round her shoulders. "But it can't be anything
serious," she said gently. "If it was they'd have found it.
It's probably just shock."

Mrs. Loftus flashed her a tremulous smile. "That's
what my husband keeps telling me. But I have a dreadful
feeling it may not be as simple as that. If there was anything specifically wrong we could do something to help
him, but as it is there's nothing, nothing. All we can do is
wait and see what happens." She glanced towards the
airport offices. "My husband wanted to tell Melanie
straightaway, but I thought it would be kinder if she
heard it from someone who isn't a stranger to her."

"I'm glad you didn't tell her, Mrs. Loftus. She's so
highly strung that I'm not sure how she'll take it."

27

"Melanie can't let my boy down!" the woman broke in. "If you only knew how he's looking forward to seeing her again! It would break his heart if she didn't go to him."

"She'll go to him all right," Loris said comfortingly, but wondered in her heart how long Melanie would have the courage to stay.

If this thing happened to her — if it had been Brett instead of Dickson — her heart contracted at the thought — she knew nothing in the world would alter her feelings for him; that if he were maimed or blinded or disfigured in any way nothing would change her love for him. But with Melanie she was not so sure. The girl had never been allowed to grow up. She had always been so protected and cosseted that Loris found herself praying that the burden she would have to bear would not prove too much for her.

She stood silent for a moment, then said quietly: "Let me break the news to her in my own way, will you? I'll leave it till we get to California, I think, because I don't want to give her too long to brood before she actually sees him."

Mrs. Loftus heaved a sigh of relief. "I don't know what I'd have done without you, my dear. It's certainly a godsend you came along with Melanie."

At that moment Melanie and Mr. Loftus came back and they all moved across the field to the waiting plane.

Flying through the night in the huge aircraft which took them nearer their destination with every passing moment, Lois remembered she had not had a chance to tell Brett she would not be staying in New York as planned. Too late now to wish she had sent him a telegram from the airport!

She lay there, thinking of him, trying to remember the fragmentary details he had given her about himself. All she knew was that his estate adjoined the Loftuses' and that he had moved there from Virginia when the doctors had advised his father to live in California. The old man

28

had died when Brett was eighteen and he had left college to go into the family business, but what this was he had not told her.

The plane hummed on steadily through the darkness and one by one the passengers turned off their lights and pushed down the backs of their seats so that they could recline more comfortably. Loris looked down at Melanie, already asleep beside her, and felt a tug of compassion as she drew the blanket over her.

One of the air hostesses passed down the gangway and leaned over to ask if there was anything she wanted, but she smilingly shook her head and settled down to try to sleep. The dim light from the roof lit the centre aisle of the plane and the noise of the engines reverberated insistently. Every now and then Loris was jerked into wakefulness by a sudden lurch of the aircraft and experienced a horrible sensation of falling. The night seemed interminable and she tried to occupy her mind by reliving the lovely days on the boat, days of idyllic happiness that seemed a dream.

"Oh, Brett," her heart cried out, "I wish you were with me, my darling," and she longed to be able to put her head against his shoulder and let him soothe away the foreboding that filled her.

CHAPTER III

IT was a clear morning when the graceful silver airliner touched down on the tarmac of Los Angeles Airport. Although it was still early, the sun was quite strong and Loris felt its warmth on her face as she stepped out of the plane. Melanie, her eyes still heavy with sleep, looked eagerly about her for a first glimpse of Dickson, and seeing her expectancy Loris was filled with apprehension at the thought of the unenviable task ahead of her. Mr. and Mrs. Loftus made some pretence of surprise that Dickson was not there to meet them, and although Melanie pouted with annoyance she seemed to be taken in by the dissimulation.

However, a long, grey, chauffeur-driven Cadillac was there to fetch them and they got in and drove off immediately. The Loftus home was in the Bel Air district, a new residential area verging on Beverly Hills, where well-to-do business people lived, and as the airport was some fourteen miles outside the city limits the drive ahead of them was a long one. The city sprawled over such a wide area that it was some time before they had crossed even a section of it, but at last the car turned in at a pair of massive wrought-iron gates and drove up a long, curved drive-way flanked by tall evergreens, until eventually the house came into view.

It was the sort of house Loris had only seen in illustrated magazines – a large, white building with a flat roof and many windows. To one side was a swimming pool with gaily coloured deck chairs set around its edges, but she only caught a glimpse of it before they drew up at the double front door. It was immediately flung open by a little boy, who dashed down the two shallow steps and threw himself into Mr. Loftus's arms.

"Hiya, Timothy!" Edward Loftus patted the child's

fair head. "Come along and be introduced to the ladies." He drew him forward and presented him in turn to Melanie and Loris. "This is Timothy, my grandson. Say how do you do, Timmy."

Loris judged the little fellow to be between eight and nine years old. He was a sturdy, rather solemn child with a mass of fair hair which he continually shook back with a toss of his head, and she was amused by the self-possession and authority with which he proceeded to direct the chauffeur to bring in their cases.

They went into the large square hall and Mrs. Loftus led them up the wide, carpeted staircase and along a light-filled corridor into the rooms she had prepared for them. "I expect you'll want to wash and tidy before you come down and see Dickson," she said kindly. "I'm sure you could do with another breakfast, too, but if you don't want to eat again there'll be coffee waiting for you in the lounge." Then, with a smile for Melanie and a quick, anxious look at Loris, she left them alone.

They spent the next few minutes removing the stains of travel. Loris was drying her hands when Melanie dashed into the bathroom. "Hurry up, Loris – you haven't got to make yourself pretty for your fiancé!"

With a heavy heart Loris followed her into her bedroom, where the girl was combing her hair.

"Melanie, there's something I've got to tell you."

"Oh, Loris, must you talk to me now – can't it wait? I'm so excited I couldn't possibly concentrate on anything serious."

Loris patted the bed. "Come and sit down just for a moment."

At the sight of Loris's grave expression Melanie reluctantly seated herself beside her. "What's the matter, old girl? Do be quick."

Loris moistened her lips. "Darling, weren't you surprised when Dickson didn't meet us in New York?"

"Of course I was, but you heard Mrs. Loftus say why he couldn't."

"I know, but didn't you think he'd be at the airport this morning?"

"Loris, what are you getting at?" Melanie began to look frightened. "You're so odd. Has something happened? Doesn't Dickson want me any more?" She jumped up and twisted her hands. "Of course, that's it! You've been putting it off till now because you've been too scared to tell me. He doesn't want me any more!"

Loris laid a restraining hand on her arm. "Don't be silly, Melanie. Of course Dickson still wants you." She drew her back on to the bed. "How could you think such a thing? No, darling, there's another reason why he couldn't come to meet you."

"What other reason?" Melanie demanded.

"Well – about a week ago, he was in a car accident. No, he's all right, my dear, don't look so frightened. It's just that. . . ."

"Is he in hospital?" Melanie broke in. "Where is he? I must go to him." She tried to pull her hand away, but Loris held it tightly.

"He's not in hospital, dear, he's here – at home. He can't get around yet, though. In fact, he's. . . ." She hesitated. "He can't walk."

"What do you mean?" The small face whitened. "Is he crippled?"

"Oh, darling, don't say things like that. Of course he's not crippled. It's simply that for the time being he's lost the use of his legs. They think it's something to do with shock."

Melanie gripped Loris's arm. "He's not disfigured, is he? I mean, it doesn't show, does it? I don't think I could bear to see him if it did! Tell me it doesn't show!" She burst into tears.

Loris took the weeping girl into her arms. "It doesn't show at all, darling. There's nothing wrong with him that you can see. It's just a nervous condition and the doctors hope it'll right itself very soon. You've got to be brave, Melanie, for his sake as well as for your own."

"But I'm not brave, Loris, I'm not! You'd be different, but I can't help being what I am. I couldn't bear it if he didn't get better."

"Hush, dear, Dickson *will* get better. But it won't help him if you're upset. He's so looking forward to seeing you. You can't let him down." She stood up and pulled Melanie to her feet. "Come along, darling, bathe your face in cold water and tidy your hair again. You mustn't let Dickson see you've been crying."

A few minutes later they descended the stairs and were hesitating at the bottom, wondering in which of the rooms they would find the Loftuses, when Mr. Loftus came down the stairs behind them, and putting both his arms around their shoulders, led them across the hall. He halted outside one of the doors and looked down at Melanie.

"Dickson's in there, waiting for you. I guess you'd like to see him on your own, so Loris and I will go into the lounge and I'll have some coffee sent in to you."

Tears rose in Melanie's eyes again but she blinked them back and hesitantly pushed open the door. She stood poised for a moment on the threshold, her small figure outlined against the sunlight, then disappeared with a rush inside and Loris heard a glad cry of "Melanie!" before the door closed behind her.

Mrs. Loftus came quickly towards Loris as they entered the lounge.

"How did she take it?" she asked anxiously.

Loris could not find it in her heart to tell Dickson's mother the words Melanie had used and the instinctive selfishness of her reaction, for she had no wish to prejudice Mrs. Loftus against her.

"She was very upset at first," she said quietly, "but on the whole she took it quite well."

Mrs. Loftus breathed a sigh of relief. "Oh, thank God! I couldn't have borne it if she'd let my boy down. Thank you, my dear, for telling her. Now come along and let me introduce you to the rest of the family. You've al-

33

ready met Timothy, Elaine's little boy. This is my daughter, and her little girl."

Loris found herself being introduced to one of the most attractive women she had ever seen. Elaine Forrest was a widow of thirty-one who did not look old enough to be the mother of Timothy or little Gillian, standing behind her. She was a striking figure, taller than the average Englishwoman, and her perfectly oval face with its magnolia complexion and large tawny eyes was framed by dark auburn hair cut short and brushed close to her perfectly shaped head. She wore a plain tailored white dress with a narrow amber belt and her movements had the sinuous grace of a sleek cat.

Loris learned that Elaine's husband had been killed in Viet-Nam, and that after his death she had returned from Washington to live with her parents, who had been delighted to have her back, for with Dickson in Europe the house was quiet and empty and Elaine's children had given it life and warmth.

Loris felt her hand taken in a light, cool grasp and when the woman spoke her voice was indifferent and polite, rather as though she were fulfilling a duty which although not irksome, was hardly a pleasure.

"How do you do, Miss Cameron? I hope you had a good trip? Guess this business about Dickson" – she waved a hand in the air – "must have come as rather a shock to you."

Loris murmured a non-committal reply and Elaine sat down and lit a cigarette while Mrs. Loftus motioned Loris to sit beside her on the couch as a coloured maid brought in coffee and hot rolls.

Melanie came out of Dickson's room to join the rest of the family for lunch and seemed to be in a subdued frame of mind. Loris watched her anxiously during the meal, but everybody went out of their way to be kind, even Elaine exerting herself and offering to show her the grounds after lunch.

"I'll go and sit with Dickson for a while," Loris

volunteered. "I haven't seen him yet and it'll be a good opportunity for us to get to know each other better. It'll do you good to get some air, Melanie."

Melanie seized on the suggestion, and after coffee followed Elaine out on to the terrace.

Loris went into the library where Dickson was lying, and the sight of the thin, fair-haired young man on the long invalid chair filled her with compassion. She could scarcely believe it was the same boy she had met in England, for his illness, although so recent, had already marked his face with lines of anxiety and fear and she knew how irksome he must find it being unable to move, remembering how athletic and vigorous he had been when she had known him before.

He reached out a large, bony hand and caught hers in a painful grip, his narrow face lighting up in a smile which revealed his white teeth, while his deep brown eyes momentarily lost their preoccupied expression.

"My, Loris, it's good to see you!" His twang, now that he was home again, seemed more pronounced than she had remembered it, but the boyish inflection had lost none of its charm.

"It's good to see you, too, Dickson – even if you *are* temporarily under the weather."

"That's what I call typical British understatement! Draw up a chair and tell me how Melanie behaved on the trip over. Did she flirt with all the eligible men?"

Loris gave a sly smile. "I'm afraid she had to do most of her entertaining in the cabin." Then, at his startled look: "When you get married, Dickson, you'd better not take her to sea on your honeymoon. She's such a frightful sailor." They both laughed and she sat down on a chair near his. "In any case we only met one eligible man. I believe you know him. Brett Halliday."

"Was Brett on the boat? Well, what do you know! How is the old son of a gun? He doesn't usually have much time for members of the fair sex."

"Really?" Loris hid a smile. "We met him the first

evening on board, before Melanie began to get seasick."

"Didn't lose much time, did he? Probably thought there was safety in numbers! Guess he made himself scarce when you were on your own, though."

"On the contrary," she said demurely, "we saw a great deal of each other."

Dickson whistled. "Congratulations! The only other woman I've never known him run away from is Elaine." Loris digested this remark in silence. "As a matter of fact," Dickson went on, "there was a time when we all thought Elaine would marry him. She certainly wasn't averse to the idea."

"And Brett?" Loris's voice was eager in spite of herself.

"Oh, nobody ever knows what goes on inside *him*! You can know him for years without finding out what makes him tick."

"But he's an old friend of yours, isn't he?"

"Gee, yes. And one of the best. Why, I remember. . . ." He broke off as Melanie came flying into the room.

She planted a swift kiss on his cheek and ruffled his hair. "What are you two looking so conspiratorial about?"

"Darling!" Dickson pulled her down against his chair and buried his face in her curls, and seeing the look of adoration which transfigured his face Loris slipped quietly out of the room.

Dinner was over and the purple sky pierced with stars when Elaine offered to show Loris the garden. "Not that you'll be able to see much of it in the dark, but we can stroll as far as the pool," she said casually. "It looks rather nice by moonlight."

Although not particularly eager to accept Elaine as her guide, Loris was glad enough to leave the sultry lounge for a while, for the heavy scent of the flowers which banked the room made her head ache, and she followed Elaine through the open veranda windows and along the terrace.

36

Without speaking they walked across the lawn and down a narrow path leading to the pool. In the moonlight it looked mysterious, and the water rippling darkly over the shining tiles distorted them into grotesque shapes, making them look like a shoal of ghostly fish.

Elaine halted at the water's edge and took out a slim, gold cigarette case. "Smoke?"

"No, thank you. I don't."

Drawing out a small lighter Elaine flicked it into life. For an instant the flame shone startlingly on her scarlet-tipped fingers, then with a snap she closed it and slipped it into her pocket, inhaling deeply and watching the smoke curl up into the still air.

"Melanie tells me you met a friend of mine on the way over."

"You mean Brett Halliday?"

"Yes. You saw quite a lot of one another, it seems. What did you think of him?" She studied the tip of her cigarette.

"I – we thought he was very charming." Loris said hesitantly.

"He can be, when it suits him. But those Atlantic crossing are so tedious, aren't they?"

"I didn't think so. But then I've never been abroad before."

"Sweet innocence! I guess Brett must have found you amusing."

"I hope he did," Loris said stiffly.

"If I know him, he didn't let the grass grow under his feet."

"What are you trying to insinuate, Mrs. Forrest?" In the darkness Loris flushed.

"Insinuate? My dear, why should you think I'm insinuating anything?"

There was a tremor in Loris's voice. "Because I don't believe you brought me out here just to show me the pool."

In that instant Elaine realized she had underestimated

the girl's intelligence. Shy and demure she might be, but she was certainly no fool. She should have remembered that Brett did not suffer fools gladly, and made a mental note to tread more warily in future.

She lowered her eyelids and studied her cigarette again. "Well, if you want the truth, Miss Cameron, I'll give it to you. Since my husband was killed Brett's been the only man I've cared about. If it hadn't been for him I couldn't have got through these last five years. You're very young yet and you don't know the meaning of loneliness. Brett made me want to go on living when I didn't care if I died." She half lifted her eyes and glanced covertly at Loris to see what effect she was having. "I never thought I'd care for anyone again, but Brett means all the world to me, and as far as I know he feels the same way."

"Why are you telling me all this, Mrs. Forrest?"

"Because I don't want you to make a fool of yourself over him. I know him so well that I can understand his every mood, but you – why, you're only a girl, and a man like Brett needs to be handled by a woman." She dropped her cigarette and trod it out with the high heel of her shoe.

"I assure you I'm quite capable of looking after myself."

Elaine shrugged. "Have it your own way, then – but don't say I didn't warn you."

Although aware of the challenge in the woman's tone, Loris did not reply and followed her in silence as she turned away from the pool, and walked through the garden to the house. After the darkness outside, the bright lights of the lounge made Loris's head ache again and she soon murmured her apologies and went to her room.

What if Elaine had been speaking the truth and Brett had only been amusing himself with her on the boat? But surely, if there was anything between him and Elaine he would not have behaved as he had – or would he?

Having an understanding with one woman would not prevent some men from becoming involved with another. But not Brett, surely not Brett! She trusted him too implicitly to believe that. If only he were here he would soon banish all her doubts, set her fears at rest and make her as happy as she had been with him that last night on the boat!

Loris got into bed and turned out the light, but the confusion of her thoughts kept her awake until far into the night.

CHAPTER IV

IN the days that followed Melanie spent most of her time talking or reading to Dickson and her companionship made him less irritable, although he chafed at having to lie like a log, unable to show his fiancée the beauties of his beloved California – the heavy waves breaking on the beach at Santa Monica, the arid desert which lay within a stone's throw of the city, and the wonderful sweet-smelling orange groves with their masses of bloom and foliage. He did not want Melanie to refuse the invitations of people who offered to show her around but was jealously possessive of her and afraid that among her escorts she might meet someone she would prefer to him. His idleness made him more introspective than was natural to him and gradually he came to realize how superficial his knowledge of Melanie was. His enforced inactivity sometimes made him hasty and evoked flashes of temper which he afterwards regretted, but although he knew his attitude could only alienate Melanie he could not help himself, and after the first few days started to watch for signs of restlessness on her part, ready to pounce on any telltale word or gesture.

Melanie sensed this and at first went out of her way to keep him amused. It was a novelty to her to play the part of a modern Florence Nightingale and she threw herself as a martyr, longing to be able to escape to the city or the beaches, which were so near and yet so tantalizingly out of reach.

Loris sensed what Dickson was going through and tried to explain it to Melanie.

"But why on earth should he be jealous?" Melanie expostulated. "I'm never out of his sight for more than a few minutes. The only time I've been out at all has been with his parents or Elaine. After all, he can't expect me to stay with him the whole day."

"I'm sure he doesn't want you to do that. But you must see it from his point of view, Melanie. After all, it isn't very pleasant for him to know that other people are showing you all the things he wanted to show you himself."

"Well, it's not very pleasant for me, either. All I've heard since I've been here is what Dickson thinks and what Dickson wants. No one bothers about me. How do you think I feel having to do everything without him? Do you think I enjoy going out with his family all the time?"

"I can understand how you feel, darling. But it isn't true to say nobody bothers about you. Dickson's parents have gone out of their way to make you feel at home."

"Oh, I know they have, Loris, and I'm not ungrateful. It's just that everything's such a disappointment. It's not a bit like I imagined it would be."

"Things are very rarely what one imagines they'll be," Loris said drily. "But you're still Dickson's fiancée and he has a right to expect you to be with him."

"But not all the time," Melanie persisted. "We'll only get on each other's nerves if I am."

"What's all this about nerves?" They both turned round startled as Mrs. Loftus came into the room. "You're too young to talk about nerves, Melanie, dear – isn't she, Loris?" Then, without waiting for a reply, she went on: "My husband and I have been thinking of giving a party for you. There are so many of Dickson's friends you haven't met yet that we thought it'd be a good idea if we invited some of them over one evening. We did intend holding a dance when you arrived, but that'll have to wait. At least you can meet some of the young people and get to know them."

"That'll be lovely!" Melanie said excitedly. "Does Dickson know?"

Mrs. Loftus put her hand to her mouth. "Oh, dear,

he wanted to tell you himself! It was his idea and now I've spoilt the surprise."

"No, you haven't, Mother Loftus. I'll pretend I don't know anything about it." Melanie danced out of the room and Mrs. Loftus looked after her affectionately.

"She's a high-spirited little thing, isn't she?" she sighed, turning to Loris. "How do you think things are going between them? I've had a feeling that Melanie hasn't been too happy. Do you think she's homesick?"

Loris pounced eagerly on that explanation. "Well, I'm sure she misses her parents."

Mrs. Loftus looked relieved. "As long as it isn't anything else," she said. "I've been worried about her."

Loris forbore to say that she had also been worrying about Melanie. Mrs. Loftus had enough to bear without adding to her anxieties.

Loris was glad to occupy her mind with Melanie, for it gave her less time to brood about herself and Brett. As soon as she had arrived in California she had written him a short note explaining why they had not stayed in New York, but re-reading it before she sent it was dismally aware it seemed all too brief and impersonal. Although she longed to be able to write all she felt she was too shy to put even the slightest endearment down on paper for her love was still too new and untried to put it into black and white, and she hoped Brett knew her well enough to read between the lines.

Eagerly each morning she awaited the arrival of the post, but no reply came, and when a week had passed and she still had not heard from him tried to find excuses for his silence. Perhaps he had found so much work awaiting him after his absence in Europe that he had not had time to write? But even as she sought excuses Loris knew in her heart that she had at least expected him to telephone. She longed to see him, yet was half afraid that when he saw her away from the glamorous background of the ship he would lose interest in her, and that in his own surroundings among the people he knew, he would find her dull and immature.

After that first evening she saw very little of Elaine, for the woman never attempted to speak to her on her own again. Sometimes at lunch or dinner Loris would catch the tawny eyes fixed speculatively upon her, although as soon as she met them they would drop, veiled by the long, dark lashes.

The party provided a welcome release from tensions for them all, and Loris was glad of the diversion.

Dickson's friends were charmed by both the English girls and particularly by Melanie. They admired Loris, they found her aloof and were too unimaginative to realize that she was only shy. Melanie had no such inhibitions and entered so wholeheartedly into the party spirit that she was soon accepted as one of the gang. Her eyes sparkled with excitement and her happy laugh pealed out continually as she flitted between Dickson's chair and his guests.

Dancing with a tow-haired young man who regaled her with accounts of his prowess on the baseball pitch, Loris watched Melanie half in amusement, half affectionately, and wished with all her heart that she had the same ability to merge her personality with others. Suddenly she could bear the bright lights and noise no longer. With a murmured apology she excused herself from her partner and slipped out on to the terrace where she rested her head against the stone balustrade and breathed and breathed in the cool air.

In this exotic part of America, with its magnificent homes, smartly dressed women and indolent, casual men, she felt like an alien, drab and colourless against their flamboyance. Even the weather seemed vulgarly perfect, with its clear, bright sunshine during the day and cool, fresh evenings. Nowhere in the world, Loris thought, could there be a climate more ideal for people with money, for here one had the best of both worlds.

Not wanting to go back into the noisy, smoky room she had just left, she descended the terrace steps into the garden, intending to stroll round to the front of the house and slip up to her room unnoticed.

Above the clamour in the lounge Elaine heard the shrill peal of the telephone. It rang so long that eventually she went out into the hall, and closing the door behind her, picked up the receiver. It was Brett.

Her mind worked quickly. Although she had tried to make Loris believe that his interest in her had been merely one of propinquity, Elaine had learned enough from Melanie to realize that this was not the case, and knew as soon as she heard Brett's voice that he had rung up to speak to Loris.

He proved her right, for after inquiring after the family in general and Dickson in particular, he asked for her.

"Hold the line a minute, Brett, I'll go and look for her."

Elaine covered the mouthpiece with one hand, slowly took out a cigarette and lit it, then picked up the receiver again.

"I guess you're out of luck. She must have gone out in the garden with one of the boys. We're throwing a party for Melanie and they haven't been free for a minute all evening. I'll ask her to call you back as soon as she comes in."

Out of the corner of her eye she saw the hall door open and Loris appear, but she pretended to be unaware of her and went on with the conversation.

"Sweet of you to call, Brett dear. When are you coming home?"

Loris stiffened at the mention of Brett's name and involuntarily moved towards the telephone, but Elaine went on as though she was not there.

"O.K., honey, I won't forget. Look after yourself, and come home soon."

She replaced the receiver and then pretended to notice Loris for the first time. "Oh, that was Brett. He's still in New York. Wasn't it sweet of him to call me?"

Loris felt her heart contract, and hardly aware of what

44

reply she made, turned blindly to go to her room and was half-way up the stairs when Elaine called after her.

"By the way, Brett sent you his regards."

Loris pretended not to hear, and when she reached the top of the stairs ran into her bedroom and threw herself on the bed in a passion of weeping, although she knew that no tears could wash away the hurt she had just received.

CHAPTER V

ONCE Melanie had met Dickson's friends she was inundated by telephone calls and invitations. At first she refused them all, but eventually even Dickson urged her not to.

"You go ahead, baby – I don't expect you to stay cooped up with me all the time. Just because I'm tied to this darned chair I don't want to make a prisoner of you. Go ahead and enjoy yourself. I don't mind as long as you come back to me."

Melanie threw her arms round his neck. "Oh, Dickson, I *would* like to see some of the sights. I know we'll be living here when we're married, but everything's so new and exciting just now."

He smiled up at her indulgently. "Then run along and have a good time, my poppet."

To start with Dickson was pleased that Melanie was enjoying herself, but after a week or so he became restive and hurt that she spent so little time with him; whenever he wanted her she seemed to be out with one or other of his friends.

Realizing the cause of Dickson's growing tension and moodiness Loris tried to warn Melanie one afternoon as she was getting ready to go out, but the girl paid no heed to her.

"Oh, Loris, we've been through all that before. Anyway, I didn't ask him if I could go out, he *told* me to go."

"Perhaps he didn't mean you to take it quite so literally? After all, you've been out every evening this week."

Melanie put down her hairbrush with a clatter.

"I don't see why you should boss me any more," she said, hotly. Then seeing the look of hurt on Loris's face, relented as quickly as she had flared up. "I'm sorry, Loris, I didn't mean that. But you know I'm not the sort

46

of person to sit doing nothing all day. I get so bored if I have to be with Dickson the whole time, and when I'm bored it makes me bad-tempered and we end up snapping at each other."

"But don't you think you should at least. . . ."

"Can't stop now, pet." She picked up her handbag. "There's a car coming up the drive and I think it's someone calling for me."

Melanie disappeared in a whirl of skirt, leaving Loris to tidy the disorderly room. With a sigh she picked up the damp towels from the bathroom floor and straightened the dressing-table in the bedroom, then slowly went downstairs and out through the lounge on to the terrace. To the left the pool shimmered in the sunlight and to her right a mass of early summer roses bloomed in a riot of colour. Dickson was lying on his chair in the middle of the lawn, shaded from the heat of the sun by a large, gaily coloured umbrella, and he looked up and waved as she appeared.

"Hallo there! What are you doing on your own? Thought you'd gone out with Melanie."

Loris went down the steps and crossed the lawn, her feet making no sound in their white flat-heeled sandals. "It's too hot to be energetic," she answered with a smile.

"Don't you find it boring doing nothing?"

"Why should I? After rainy England, this is paradise!"

"Even paradise can be sickening after a time."

She was shocked at the bitterness in his tone. "Oh, Dickson, don't talk like that. You've got so much to be thankful for."

"Sure," he said bitterly. "I'm a cripple, engaged to a beautiful girl. I've got a lot to be thankful for. How long do you think I'll be able to keep Melanie if I can't walk?"

"When you say things like that you're only hurting yourself, Dickson. Melanie loves you."

He laughed shortly. "I'm not doubting that – yet – but how long do you think she'll go on loving like this?" He

47

pointed to his recumbent body. "No, Loris, I'm not kidding myself any longer. If I don't get well soon, I'll never be able to marry her." Then he shrugged and attempted a grin. "But that's enough about my troubles. Tell me what you think of California."

"You're the umpteenth person to ask me that," Loris smiled, "but I haven't seen enough of it yet to give you an answer." She moved over to the deck chair by his side and picked up a book which was lying on the seat. "Hallo, what's this? Oh, *War and Peace*. Haven't you read it either?"

"I didn't get much time for reading before my accident. Matter of fact, it's only since the accident that I've realized how many books there are in the world!"

"I didn't have much time for reading at home either. Would you like me to read to you?"

"I'd sure appreciate it if you would," he said eagerly. "But you'll probably be old and grey before you've finished it!"

"That's a chance I'll have to take." She sat down smiling and began to read.

Occasionally her voice was drowned by the heavy drone of aircraft overhead and she looked up once or twice to watch them as they flew towards the airport, little knowing that one of them was to carry Brett to Los Angeles that afternoon.

When Brett had telephoned the Plaza Hotel on the evening the ship docked, he had been surprised to hear that the reservations for Dickson, Melanie and Loris had been cancelled, and had presumed they had decided to go straight out to California. For the first two or three days he was so inundated with work that he had no time to answer Loris's note, although he carried it around with him in his wallet. But on the fourth evening of his stay in New York he was able to make the long-distance call to Los Angeles which Elaine had answered, and had been acutely disappointed when she had told him Loris could not come to the phone. He had replaced the receiver with a feeling of frustration, buoyed up with the anticipation of speaking to her within a few hours at the most; but as that night passed and the next few days, he had been perplexed at not hearing from her, never guessing for a moment that Elaine had not given Loris his message – had not in fact even told her that he had telephoned with the sole intention of speaking to her. He longed to get back to California and find out what was wrong, but business delayed him in New York longer than he had anticipated, and it was more than a fortnight before he was able to take a plane for the west coast.

Elaine managed quite successfully to combat her slight feeling of guilt at not giving Loris Brett's message, and the sight of the girl's unhappy face only served to antagonize her with its unwitting reproach. Although she did not know when Brett was returning she made up her mind to meet him at the airport and racked her brains for some way to find out when he was arriving.

It was Timothy who solved the problem for her. The little boy had formed a deep attachment for Brett, and loved to visit Brett's colonial-style house standing on a wooded slope about a mile from the Loftus home. One morning at breakfast he suddenly remembered Brett had promised him one of the puppies his spaniel Belle was due to produce, and asked his mother to take him over to see if they had arrived.

Unexpectedly, Elaine kissed her little son. "Of course, darling. I'll take you over this morning."

They drove to Brett's house before lunch, and while Timothy ran round the back to ask the gardener to show him the litter, Elaine sauntered up the front steps into the cool hall. She found Dorcas, Brett's coloured butler, industriously polishing the hall table.

"You're busy today, Dorcas. Expecting Mr. Brett?"

"Yassum. Mis' Brett's arriving on the afternoon plane. Cable came from him last night, and we got to work fast to get everything ready. Ah'll sho' be glad to see him back."

Elaine's heart beat a triumphant tattoo. "I'll be near the airport this afternoon," she said casually, "so I can meet him and you needn't bother to send the car."

She was descending the steps as Timothy came running to meet her.

"Have you got the pup you wanted, honey?" she asked kindly.

"No, Mummy. The gardener says I can't have it yet as it's too little to leave its mother – so I'll have to wait."

"Never mind, you can always come back for it in a few weeks' time. I'm sure Uncle Bett'll keep it for you."

She helped the disappointed little boy into the car and sent the long, low Packard gliding down the drive.

As Brett stepped out of the plane he was surprised to see Elaine waiting for him. She came towards him, cool and soignée, and held up her cheek so naturally for his kiss that for an instant his lips lay on her soft skin.

"Hallo there, Elaine, good to see you after all this time. How've you been?" Then without waiting her answer: "What are you doing here, though – meeting someone?"

"Only you," she laughed up at him. "I took Timothy over to your place for the puppy you promised him, and Dorcas told me you were expected this afternoon. You wretch, why didn't you write me you were coming?"

Brett laughed easily. "Since when could I presume on your time?"

As they spoke, his eyes searched the waiting crowd, hoping Elaine had told Loris she was going to meet him, but there was no sign of her and he had no option but to follow Elaine to her car.

"It's good to be back," he said as he settled himself in his seat.

"I didn't think you missed us."

"I always miss my friends. Incidentally, how's Dickson? Can he walk yet?"

50

Elaine shot him a swift glance as she started the car. "No, he's still laid up."

"How did Melanie take it?" Brett asked.

"She was quite good at first, but she's too young to stay cooped up with an invalid all the time. You know how impatient Dickson always was, and his illness hasn't improved him any. Things weren't too bad until the party, but as soon as his crowd started rushing her she lost her head completely. He resented her going out without him at all to begin with, but as soon as he gave her a little leeway she took him at his word and he's hardly seen anything of her since. Which, of course, was just the chance little Miss Cameron was waiting for."

Brett jerked his head round at the mention of Loris's name. "What do you mean?"

Elaine laughed lightly. "What sort of chance does an unattached girl usually wait for?" she asked.

"When I met her on the boat she certainly didn't strike me as that type," he countered.

Elaine looked at him sideways. "Men are notoriously bad judges of character, my dear. You were probably fooled by her innocent appearance, like the rest of us. But she's certainly not my idea of a friend. You'd think that knowing how jealous Dickson is she'd try to persuade Melanie to spend more time with him. But no. Whenever Melanie's out, which is nearly all the time, these days, Loris is only too eager to take her place. And that's not *my* idea of friendship." She drew the car up at the traffic lights. "Got a cigarette for me, Brett?"

"Huh?" Roused from his thoughts, he reached abstractedly into his pocket and offered her one. They smoked in silence, Elaine perfectly content now that she had told him what she wanted him to believe – content in the knowledge that she had planted a seed of doubt in his mind and that his own natural jealousy would inevitably fan it into life.

She had met Brett for the first time shortly after her husband's death and had been instantly attracted by his

51

intense, dark looks and air of sophisticated detachment. The fact that he obviously did not look upon her as more than a friend only made her more determined to penetrate his reserve and she had become obsessed with the idea of getting him, her vanity making her refuse to believe that any man could remain impervious to her attractions for very long.

For his part, Brett was well aware that he had only to ask Elaine to marry him and she would accept with alacrity. Many women had tried to inveigle him into marriage, but he had evaded them all, looking beneath their superficial glamour for something they were usually incapable of giving. Their avariciousness had sickened him, and although he had occasionally amused himself with girls who had found the idea of becoming Mrs. Brett Halliday an attractive one, he had tired of them after a few weeks and sought distraction in some other lovely face.

But in Loris he thought he had at last found what he was seeking. When he had first seen her in her simple, dark dress, looking like a schoolgirl among the sophisticated women in the cocktail bar, he had felt instinctively that he could trust her. The idealist in him refused to let him believe that his first impression had been wrong, yet that part of him which was cynical, his wary attitude to life and to women in particular – an attitude which experience had done nothing to dispel – made him pay more attention to Elaine's insinuations than he might otherwise have done.

"Do you want to go straight home, Brett," Elaine asked suddenly, "or will you come over and see Dickson first? I know he'd love it. You could have a drink with him and then I'd drive you back."

In spite of himself Brett's spirits rose at the possibility of seeing Loris. "O.K., Elaine – good idea."

When the car swung into the drive and halted in front of the house, they got out and mounted the steps together.

"Come on through, Brett. Dickson's probably in the garden."

Following her through the lounge and out on to the terrace, his eyes jumped instantly to the man and girl sitting on the lawn with a book between them, and jealousy stabbed him at the sight of the dark head almost touching the fair one.

Elaine's high heels clicked on the terrace and Loris looked up. Her face lit up with joy when she saw Brett, but the smile on her lips trembled at the sight of Elaine's slim arm resting possessively in his.

"Hallo, you two – look who I've brought home with me!" Elaine's tone was triumphant. "His plane was nearly half an hour late – and how I *hate* waiting around for people to arrive. . . ."

Loris stiffened. So Brett had told Elaine the time of his arrival but had not let her know! Her smile of welcome froze on her face, but she greeted him with composure. Brett gave her a searching look as they shook hands, but she refused to meet his eyes and he wondered whether she was embarrassed because he had found her and Dickson together. He longed to say something to her, but Dickson was looking up at him quizzically and Brett leant over and took his hand.

"Well, you're a fine surprise, I must say! How'd you manage it?"

The two men started to talk and presently Elaine disappeared into the house. Loris drew her chair a little apart, picked up the book and pretended to read, but Brett, watching her covertly, knew it was mere pretence, for she did not turn over a single page. Her gesture of withdrawal chilled him and he told himself bitterly that Elaine had apparently been right. If Loris intended to show him that what had happened between them on the boat meant nothing to her, she was succeeding only too well.

A few moments later Elaine came back bearing a tray with four glasses of iced Tom Collins which she handed round, and Loris came back into the group to take hers. As they drank, Elaine and Dickson questioned Brett about his trip to Europe, and Loris assumed a listening attitude although she did not join in the conversation.

"It's certainly grand to have you back," Dickson said. "We've all missed you stopping by for a drink in the evening. And," he cracked humorously, "it took Elaine at least a week to find a new escort!"

"I'm flattered it took as long as that," Brett responded gallantly. "I wouldn't have said she needed more than three days at most."

Elaine yawned. "Quit the teasing, boys, or Loris'll think I'm really as fickle as you make it sound." She stood up and smoothed her skirt down over her slim hips. "Come along, honey, I'll drive you back."

Brett got to his feet. "I'll be over to see you again as soon as I get settled, Dickson old son. Then we can have a pow-wow and smoke a pipe of peace. Tell Melanie I'm sorry I missed seeing her. Now I'm back I want to give a party for you both, but more about that later, huh?"

With a friendly nod to Dickson and a cool smile for Loris he moved away. Loris could hardly believe he was leaving without a word as to when they would meet again; his impersonal attitude hurt her more than anything he could have said or done, and tears pricked her eyes as she watched his retreating figure.

"Brett didn't have much to say to you, did he? I thought you knew him rather well," Dickson said chaffingly.

"I thought I did, too," Loris murmured.

"He certainly handed you the frozen mitt. I told you he was unpredictable, didn't I?"

"You were right." Forcing a smile to her lips, she sat down and picked up the heavy book, bending her eyes over it so that he should not see the expression in her eyes. "We've got an awful lot of this to get through, Dickson. Shall I go on reading?"

CHAPTER VI

TRY as she would Loris could make no sense out of her encounter with Brett. Although everything seemed to show that the insinuations Elaine had made to her that evening by the pool were true, she could not bear to believe that Brett had merely been amusing himself with her, and tried to find some reason for his coolness.

When he had left with barely a nod she had half expected him to telephone and arrange to meet her to bring out in the open whatever it was that had set up this barrier between them. As day followed day and she still did not hear from him the hope she was cherishing began to die, although she jumped every time the telephone rang and would sit with a strained expression on her face until she heard that the call was not for her.

Had it not been for Melanie Loris would have returned home immediately, but she felt under an obligation to stay with her friend until the situation between Dickson and her was settled. Things had not been going well with the young couple, for Dickson was becoming increasingly jealous of Melanie's preoccupation with his friends, and in particular with a young Argentinian called Miguel Santos who was in California on business, but found time to take Melanie out nearly every day.

Even Loris was assailed by misgivings at Melanie's friendship with this young man. But she did not think it wise to intervene, knowing how resentful Melanie was at any interference in her affairs.

One night, a week after Brett's return to California, she knew she could no longer bear being so near him without seeing him, and decided to book her passage home.

She went down to breakfast next morning relieved that her decision was made and had her meal alone in the dining-room. Elaine and Mrs. Loftus breakfasted in their bedrooms and only Loris and Mr. Loftus shared the dining-room, for Melanie usually rushed down so late that they were already finished. After she had eaten the crisp white rolls and boiled eggs served in a wine-glass topped with a creamy mound of butter, she went into the library and chose a book at random, her mind too preoccupied to lose itself in anything.

She was walking through the hall on her way into the garden when she heard the slamming of an upstairs door and looked up to see Elaine coming downstairs.

"Good morning," she called briefly.

Elaine gave her a cool smile and ran down the last few stairs. "Going into the garden?" she asked, glancing down at the book.

"Yes. I thought I might as well get as much sun as I can while I'm still here."

"Oh?" Elaine raised thin, arched eyebrows. "Are you thinking of leaving us, then?"

"Yes."

"Don't you like it here?"

Loris ignored the faintly mocking note in the drawling voice. "Very much, but I can't go on accepting your parents' hospitality indefinitely. Of course I'd love to stay, if only to see Melanie – I mean, to –"

"To see Melanie safely married?"

"Yes," Loris said honestly. "Still, I expect things will work out when I've gone."

"But why be in such a hurry?"

Loris hesitated to tell her the real reason, but did not wish Elaine to think she was running away from Brett. "To be frank, Mrs. Forrest, I'm running out of money, and America is the last country in the world where one can stay without money."

While only too eager to get Loris out of the way, Elaine was shrewd enough to realize that when Brett heard she was leaving he might decide to see her before she left to try and clear up the misunderstanding between them. Far better for Loris to leave when the mistrust had deepened and it would take more than one meeting to bring them together again. Suddenly an idea came to her, an idea by means of which she could act the Good Samaritan and at the same time keep the girl more or less under her control.

"Come into the dining-room while I pour myself out some coffee, Loris. I'd like to talk to you."

She led the way in silence and it was only when she was seated at the table with a cup of steaming black coffee before her and the inevitable cigarette in her hand that she turned her attention to Loris again.

"I know you're not very happy about Melanie, so if you'd like to stay on, I can offer you a job."

"A job?" Loris echoed.

"Yes. Timothy and Gillian are on my hands at the moment, as you probably know. Until a few weeks ago I had a governess to look after them, but as they're both going to boarding-school in September it didn't seem worth while getting anyone else when she had to leave – although," she made a grimace, "if I'd known how troublesome they were, I'd have thought twice about it. I was going to get a temporary nanny to take care of them, but what you've just said has given me an idea. How would you like to look after them for me? I'll pay you the usual salary, of course."

Loris was surprised at the offer, sure that Elaine would have rejoiced at her departure. One look at the woman's face with its pouting mouth and veiled, secretive eyes made her instantly dismiss from her mind the idea that Elaine was offering her a job out of compassion. That she had a reason for her magnanimity Loris was sure, although for the moment she could not see what it was. Her instinctive reaction was to refuse, but even now the thought of leaving Melanie held her back.

"I've never looked after children before. If I stay, what exactly will I have to do?"

Elaine shrugged. "Oh, the usual things. Whatever one

has to do for children. After I've seen that they've washed themselves and eaten their food I leave them pretty much to their own devices. I suppose you'd take them for walks and keep them amused – in other words, take them completely off my hands. By the time they go to school a lot of things may have changed." She blew a cloud of smoke into the air. "Well, what about it? Will you stay?"

"Yes, Mrs. Forrest. And thank you very much." Loris moved to the door and then turned, her hand on the knob. "When do you want me to start?" she asked.

"Right now would suit me." Elaine poured herself another cup of coffee and as if to establish the new relationship between them, gave Loris a nod of dismissal. With a faint smile Loris inclined her head and left the room, thinking wryly that with her first week's salary it would be as well to buy a simple white dress to serve as a uniform and make her look more in keeping with the part.

Eager to tell someone her news she ran upstairs to the bedroom where Melanie, still flushed from sleep, was just opening her eyes.

"Wake up, sleepyhead! You're later than ever this morning."

Melanie yawned and stretched luxuriantly. "There's no hurry. I'm not seeing Miguel till after lunch." She sat up and hugged her knees. "Oh, Loris, we had such a lovely time last night, and. . . ."

"And it was very late when you got home," Loris finished. "But listen to my news first. Elaine's given me a job."

"Elaine's given you a what?" The blue eyes opened in astonishment.

Loris sat down on the bed. "She's given me a job. I'm going to look after Timothy and Gillian for her and she's going to pay me the usual salary a children's nurse gets over here."

"But why? Oh, I know you like children and all that,

58

but why work for Elaine? I thought you didn't like her."

"It's not a question of likes and dislikes, my poppet," Loris said gently. "But I can't live on air, you know. I don't spend much, but do you realize my money is running low?"

"But, Loris, I'd let you –"

"I know you would, darling, and it's sweet of you. But I couldn't accept."

She stood up. "Now I'd better go down and find the children. I must get them to show me where their things are kept. I don't relish the idea of asking Elaine."

As Loris was walking out of the room, Melanie called after her: "Do I have to call you Nanny now?"

Picking up a silk slip which Melanie had discarded on the floor the night before, Loris threw it at her. "Not if you still want to be my friend."

She went downstairs again and looked for Timothy and Gillian. If she was going to work she might as well begin immediately.

She found the children playing in the garden and called to them across the lawn. They came bounding up the steps of the terrace and sat down one on either side of her on the gaily striped hammock.

"I've something to tell you," Loris said. "Your mother has asked me to look after you until you start school in September."

The little boy and girl looked at each other in silence. Then Timothy asked suspiciously: "Do you mean you're going to be our nanny? Will we have to call you that?" His tone suggested that he considered it a personal affront for a boy of nearly ten to have a nanny at all, and Loris bit back a smile.

"I'll be your nanny, but of course you can still call me Loris."

"Oh." He was somewhat mollified. "Will you take us to the beach and the shops like Miss Heflin used to?"

Presuming Miss Heflin to be her predecessor, Loris nodded. "Of course I will, Timmy. But I'll have to rely on you to show me where to go, because I'm quite a stranger here still."

"Will you tell us all about England?" It was Gillian this time. "Is it really as small as it looks on the map? And have you seen the Queen?"

Loris smiled. "It isn't *quite* as small as it looks on the map, and I'm afraid I haven't seen the Queen, dear, but I can tell you lots of nice things about her."

"I've got a photo of her," Timothy said, proudly. "My granny in Washington met her when she came over here once."

"Well, she probably knows more about her than I do, then," Loris replied.

"I guess she does, but we never get to see her, so she can't tell us," the small boy said mournfully.

"All right then, if I tell you all about the Queen, you'll have to tell me where all your things are kept and what you have to wear and what you eat."

Laughing and chattering together the children led her into the house and up to their nursery, a large airy room overlooking the garden, where they proceeded to show her where their clothes and their toys were kept. The first morning passed quickly and by the time Loris had found out all she needed to know, it was nearly time for lunch. She shepherded the children into the dining-room and Mr. Loftus greeted her with a special smile and she guessed Elaine had told him of the arrangement.

"So you're going to keep an eye on the kids!" he beamed. "Let me know if they're too much of a handful and I'll come and spank them for you."

"I hope you won't have to do that!" she laughed.

He looked at her keenly from beneath bushy eyebrows. "You know, my dear, there was no need for you to take this on. You're welcome to stay as long as you like, and you had only to come to me for anything you needed and I'd have been pleased to give it to you."

"I know, Mr. Loftus, and I can't tell you how much I appreciate it," Loris said quietly. "But I feel better now I have a job to do. I've never been used to idling and it'll be nice to have something to keep me occupied."

"It's quite a change to hear a young woman say that!" He patted her cheek. "But let me know if there's anything I can do, won't you? You needn't be shy about it."

He broke off as Mrs. Loftus and Elaine came into the room, followed by Melanie.

Lunch that day was a hurried meal, each member of the family preoccupied with their own concerns. Edward Loftus had a business appointment in the early afternoon, his wife and daughter fittings with their dressmaker, and even Melanie seemed absorbed in her own secret thoughts. As they were finishing the meal they saw Dickson being wheeled out on to the lawn below the terrace. He waved across to them gaily before the nurse turned him away from the glare of the sun.

Mr. Loftus looked down at his watch and then glanced at his wife. "My appointment's at two-thirty, so if you two want a lift you'd better be quick. I'll go on out and get the car."

Mrs. Loftus hastily drained her coffee cup. "I'm ready now, dear. How about you, Elaine?"

"I'll just go up and get my jacket." Elaine rose from the table. "Meet you outside."

Mother and daughter hurried out of the room, leaving Melanie and Loris alone at the table.

"Shall we take our coffee outside and join Dickson?" Melanie suggested.

Loris looked up in surprise, for the girl's behaviour had become increasingly casual towards her fiancé durng the last few weeks.

"I'd love to," she said.

With their cups in their hands and followed by Timothy and Gillian, they went out over the terrace across the lawn, where they arranged themselves in deck chairs around Dickson, the children sprawling lazily on the grass.

Dickson brightened at their approach, but the lines

around his eyes and mouth – lines which only a few weeks ago had been faint – had now deepened, making him look older and more mature, and although Loris thought it gave his face added strength and character, she regretted it should have been at such a price.

"You didn't come and see me this morning, Melly," he chided gently.

"Sorry, darling, but I didn't get home till very late last night and I overslept."

A shadow crossed his face, but his voice was light and infused with interest. "Did you have a good time?"

"Wonderful! Miguel took me to the divinest restaurant and we danced till our feet nearly fell off!"

Dickson jerked his head up. "Miguel again? What happened to the rest of the gang?"

"Bob and Elspeth didn't turn up at the last moment, and Janey and Phil decided to go on somewhere else instead."

"That was very convenient for you both, wasn't it?"

Melanie perched herself on the arm of his chair and ruffled his hair. "Darling, you aren't jealous, are you? You told me you didn't want me to sit at home with you all the time. If I did, I wouldn't go on being cheerful and gay or any of the things you said you fell in love with."

Dickson reached up and pulled her face to his. "Sometimes, darling, a man wants something more than just a girl who's the life and soul of the party. Because I fell in love with you when you were cheerful and gay doesn't mean you always have to act that way. Love isn't something that stands still – Melly – it changes, you know. It grows."

He spoke so seriously and with such obvious sincerity that Loris felt like a trespasser, and would have tiptoed away had she not felt that her going would have been more obvious than remaining where she was.

But his effect on Melanie was very different.

"Oh, don't be so stuffy, Dickson," she said petulantly. "You don't have to lecture me just because I enjoy myself with Miguel."

"Let's forget it, shall we?" Dickson attempted a grin. "After all, it's not important enough to argue about." But the expression in his eyes belied the lightness of his tone.

Quick to forget, Melanie gave him a swift kiss and sat down on the grass at his feet. But hardly had she settled herself when she glanced at her watch and gave an exclamation. "Heavens, I didn't know it was so late. I must fly!"

"Where are you going?" Dickson asked sharply.

"Only for a swim, darling." She scrambled to her feet.

"Good idea," he said cheerfully. "I'll get Nurse to wheel my chair to the edge of the pool and I can watch you."

"But I'm not going swimming in the pool," Melanie said, flushing.

"Where are you going, then – the beach?"

"Yes, Santa Monica. I'm going with Bob and Elspeth."

Heroically Dickson swallowed his disappointment. He had looked forward to spending the afternoon with her, for in the last weeks they had spent so little time together that he was beginning to feel they were drifting apart.

"Well, it's a lovely day for a swim. Too hot for anything else, in fact. When Bob calls for you, ask him to come out and see me for a minute or two, will you?"

Melanie dug the heel of her shoe into the grass. "Bob isn't calling for me."

"Then how are you going to get there?"

Tell-tale colour flooded her face and he went on sharply: "Don't tell me that Miguel dago is calling for you?"

"Yes, he is," she replied defiantly. "And he isn't a dago."

"Good God, Melanie, haven't you any sense at all? If you must amuse yourself while I'm ill, you might at least choose someone with a more savoury reputation."

"That's a horrible thing to say! If you can't trust me –"

"Don't let's quarrel about it," Dickson broke in stiffly. "When he calls Loris can tell him you have a headache."

"But I want to go!"

"And I don't want you to."

"I'm not going to let him down just because you're jealous. I said I'd go and I will!" Without waiting for a reply Melanie turned and fled across the lawn.

Loris stood up, stricken at the anger and hurt in Dickson's face. "I'll go after her. I'm sure she didn't mean what she said."

"Don't bother, thanks," Dickson said bitterly. "If she wants to go out that badly, let her go."

"I'll just run up and have a word with her, anyway."

She hurried into the house and found Melanie putting her coat on in the lounge.

"Well?" the girl said defiantly, turning to face her. "Have you come to preach to me, too?"

'Oh, dear,' Loris thought, 'this is going to be worse than I imagined.' Aloud, she said: "Of course not. You know I don't preach. Neither does Dickson."

"You both have a good try, though."

"But, Melanie, do you think you're being fair to him? After all, you did come out here to marry him."

"It isn't my fault that I can't."

"I know. But it isn't Dickson's fault either. He's been through such a dreadful time – you might at least try to make it up to him."

"I do try," Melanie answered sullenly. "I can't help it if he's jealous and stupid."

"It isn't stupid to be jealous. After all, it wouldn't be very flattering to you if he wasn't. And anyway, he knows Miguel better than you do."

"But he doesn't – that's the whole point. Miguel isn't a bit like Dickson thinks he is. He's always been charming to me. *He's* never tried to boss me or tell me what to do." Tears trembled on the fair lashes.

"But doesn't it worry you to think of Dickson always left on his own?"

"Dickson isn't left on his own. If I'm not here, you always are. You're always here to talk to him and keep him amused, so I'm going out with Miguel!"

Melanie turned and ran out of the room, bumping into someone who was coming in, but not pausing even to apologize.

Loris sat down, white and shaken, her eyes fixed on the man's face as he walked into the room. "Brett!"

"I seem to have come at an inopportune moment," he said icily.

Since his return to California Brett had been in a state of doubt and conflict. But after a few days the jealousy he had felt at his first sight of Loris and Dickson together had diminished, and he had realized it was only fair to give Loris a chance to explain why she had not tele- phoned him. Having decided this, he made up his mind to see her and hear from her own lips a denial of all Elaine's insinuations; so he had driven over to the house directly after lunch that day. The front door was open and he had crossed the hall and entered the room just in time to hear Melanie's outburst. The words were etched in his brain and he felt he would never forget them.

"Dickson isn't left on his own. If I'm not here, you always are. You're always here to talk to him and keep him amused, so I'm going out with Miguel!"

The sound of her sobbing as she ran out of the room still echoed in his ears and in that instant he decided that everything Elaine had said about Loris must be true.

His voice was harsh when he spoke. "Do you get any satisfaction out of trying to come between Melanie and Dickson? Wouldn't some other man do as well – if not better?"

"What do you mean?"

"Yours seems to be the sort of affection that doesn't survive a separation, even a short one. You don't flatter me by preferring Dickson."

"Preferring Dickson?" Loris echoed incredulously.

"Yes. I suppose you go by the rule that a bird in the hand is worth two in the bush?"

Loris stood up, trembling. "How dare you speak to me like that? Do you think so little of me that you couldn't even wait for an explanation? I thought I knew you, Brett, but it seems I was wrong. Were you so afraid you might be forced into marrying me that you had to pick on the first ridiculous excuse to make it impossible? If that was your intention, you've certainly succeeded!"

"You might fool someone else by those tactics, but not me," Brett said grimly.

"I wouldn't attempt to fool you," she flashed back. "I'll leave that to women like Elaine Forrest."

Brett gave an exclamation, but before he could reply Dickson called from the garden. "Is that old Brett in there with you, Loris? Tell him to come out and see me."

Without a word Brett strode past her and Loris ran upstairs and flung herself across her bed in a storm of weeping.

At last, all emotion spent, she went into the bathroom and washed her face in cold water, tidied her hair and dabbed her nose lightly with powder. Then looking at herself in the mirror to make sure no sign remained of her tears, she decided to go downstairs and behave as if nothing had happened.

She went out into the garden and saw that Elaine had joined Dickson and Brett on the lawn. They were all laughing at something Timothy had just said and did not hear her approach until Elaine suddenly looked up and caught sight of her.

"You're just in time to collect the children, my dear. They're getting tired of sitting still, so you'd better take them for a walk."

Seeming restored to humour, Dickson looked from her to Brett and grinned, "What do you think of our new nanny?"

"New nanny?" Brett queried.

"Loris is so keen to stay here," Elaine interposed. "that she's taken on the job of looking after the children until they go to school."

"I see." Brett's tone was non-committal. "Do you like the climate so much, Loris?"

"No, Brett – the people."

CHAPTER VII

"Happy birthday, Timothy!"

The little boy sat at the breakfast table surrounded by piles of gaily wrapped parcels. He was ten years old that day, and all the family had come down to breakfast so that they could share his pleasure as he unwrapped each present.

His grandparents had given him a bicycle and his mother a cowboy costume, complete to the last detail from the wide-brimmed Stetson hat to the jingling spurs. Even Melanie and Dickson had patched up their quarrel sufficiently to buy the child a joint present, while Loris had spent half her wages on a watch with a Mickey Mouse dial.

When breakfast was over Loris left the children with the family, for today was Timothy's day and he was the boss, but after lunch she got them ready for the expedition Mr. Loftus had arranged to one of the film studios. This had long been one of Timothy's dreams, and his grandfather had obtained a special pass to allow them to enter the hallowed precincts. The children were so wild with excitement that even Loris was infected by their enthusiasm and looked forward to the trip with almost as much eagerness as they did.

She had been glad, however, of the morning's respite, for she found it tiring to keep Timothy and Gillian amused all day. Unlike their English counterparts, they seemed uninterested in picture books or reading and were continually on the go, bombarding her, when lack of breath forced them to sit still, with questions about everything that came into their heads, particularly questions about England and her home. She often had to rack her brains to find the right answers, and almost forgotten facts about English history and geography came to light in her efforts to satisfy them.

In the past few weeks Loris had grown thinner and faint hollows had appeared below her cheek bones. Although careful to have a ready smile and hide her unhappy thoughts whenever she was with the family, there were times when her mask of composure fell and this did not go as unnoticed as she hoped.

For the afternoon's excursion she put on a cool white dress and tightening the narrow red belt around her waist, ran lightly down the stairs to join the children, who were waiting for her impatiently in their grandfather's car. The drive ahead was a long one, for most of the studios were situated either in Culver City, some twenty miles from Los Angeles, or in the San Fernando valley, where many of the stars owned ranches. The long gleaming white highway stretched straight as a ribbon for miles, and on either side the dusty grey hills merged into undulating plains that seemed to disappear into eternity.

The children were well behaved at first, but by the time the car nosed its way past the policeman at the gates of the wire enclosure surrounding Lion Studios they were showing signs of restlessness. They drove on past enormous hangar-like buildings until the car drew up at the entrance to the main office. Loris and the children stepped out to be met by a short, thin man with crinkly grey hair who had obviously been waiting for them.

"Are you with Mr. Loftus's grandchildren?" he asked Loris. And when she nodded, went on: "Good. My name's Al Belland, and I've been designated to show you around." He looked down at the children with a genial smile. "Well, kids, where shall we start? There's a picture on the floor at the moment which has a Christmas scene on schedule, so if we go along there we might get to see the tree all lit up. Then there's the studio canteen, where you're sure to see some of the stars, and the make-up room and wardrobe room, and lots more besides. Which shall it be first?"

Timothy and Gillian seemed taken aback by the offer of such liberality. After much whispered consultation they decided to see the canteen first and leave the film until the end, in the manner of children the world over who leave the tit-bit till last.

Loris had not realized that a studio could be so vast, and after a while found herself wishing they had the car to take them from one building to another, for it was tiring to walk along the hot concrete paths. Their way to the canteen took them through several empty lots, and they came upon a Gold Rush town complete in every detail from a gaudy saloon bar to the tethering-posts for the cowboys' horses. It lay gathering dust, exposed to the glare of the sun in one corner of the huge acreage covered by the studio, the streets and houses looking so real that it was uncanny to step behind them and discover they were merely plaster fronts supported by wooden posts. Farther along they came to an enormous empty tank, which Al explained was used for making scenes at sea, and beyond that, Eros stood in the middle of a replica of Piccadilly. It was strange to see the heart of London tucked away among the jumble of exotic sets, and Loris felt a pang of homesickness as she looked up at the plaster cast of the little god of Love.

When they reached the studio canteen Timothy recognized one of his favourite cowboy heroes, and Gillian, at the sight of a group of film extras in the clothes of a bridal party, amused everybody by piping up: "Why are they here, Loris – why don't they go to church?"

After they had rested and had some refreshment Al led them into the hot sunshine again and across to a large, squat building with a placard on the door which bore the warning: 'Silence.'

Al stuck his head round tentatively and then turned and beckoned to Loris and the children. "It's O.K. They're not shooting, so we can go in."

70

"Are they going to kill somebody?" Gillian asked earnestly.

"Not on your sweet life, little lady! That just means they're going to film a scene for the picture."

As quietly as they could they entered the huge, barn-like building, with its concrete walls and corrugated iron roof. Over to one side a series of cubicles served as dressing-rooms for the stars, and in front of one of them a girl sat before a lighted mirror, while a make-up man bent over her repairing the ravages to her make-up caused by the heat of the lights.

They walked across the floor, which was strewn with electric cables and coils of rope, and made their way to the far end, where they saw a set resembling a house. As they approached it, it proved to be only a painted front like the Gold Rush town had been, and Al led them round the back of it and showed them the rooms that had been built behind. There was a small kitchen leading into a lounge, and in it a young man and woman stood staring motionlessly at each other with expressionless faces, while a technician ran round them holding up a little gadget which Al explained was for measuring the amount of light needed for the cameras to make the next shot.

Suddenly the young man and woman walked off, to be replaced by the two stars for whom they had been acting as stand-ins. A stentorian voice yelled for silence, and instantly there was a magic quiet. Arc lights and spot lights glowed into life and the scene was lit by a fierce white glare. Loris and the children watched fascinated as the actors proceeded to rehearse the scene. Time after time they were stopped by the director, who explained how he wanted certain gestures and movements made, and Loris was amazed by the effort and patience needed to get the scene right. Eventually he seemed satisfied and gave orders for the shooting to begin. More lights went on, the microphones were lowered from the ceiling, and the cameras moved in and started to turn.

71

"Cut!" At last the scene was 'in the can' and the noise broke out again as the cameras swung back and the microphones vanished into the ceiling.

"Mind, darling, you might get in the way." Loris caught Gillian by the hand and as she pulled her back bumped into a man standing behind them.

"I beg your pardon, I didn't...." The words died away as she looked up and saw it was Brett.

"Good afternoon," he said stiffly. "I didn't expect to see you here."

"I – it's Timothy's birthday and Mr. Loftus arranged this visit as a treat for him. What are *you* doing here?" The words were out before she could stop them.

"I have an interest in these studios," he said briefly.

At that moment, Timothy, who had been inspecting one of the cameras, caught sight of Brett and came running over, and Brett bent and solemnly wished him a happy birthday. "Are you enjoying yourself, Timmy?"

"Gee, yes – but of course we've walked around an awful lot and it's very tiring for the girls." The little boy looked deprecatingly at Loris and his sister.

Brett hid a smile. "What are you going to do now?"

Loris interrupted, "We're just going home."

"Oh, Loris," Timothy complained, "you promised we could have an ice-cream before we left."

"I'll buy you one," Brett said, then turned inquiringly to Loris. "That is, if you'll let me."

Loris nodded, and Brett turned back to the children. "Come along, then, I'll take you somewhere special and you can have the biggest ice-cream they've got."

"But we've got our own car," Loris protested.

"That's all right," he said easily. "I'll send it home and take you back in mine."

They left the studio together and walked over to the car park where Brett's shining drophead Studebaker was standing. The children piled into the back excitedly and Loris had no option but to sit in front next to Brett. They drove past the studio policeman again, the man tipping his cap respectfully as he recognized the driver, turned right and then left the Wilshire Boulevard and on in the direction of Los Angeles.

"Where are we going, Uncle Brett?" Timothy shouted.

"How would you like to have your ice-cream at the Ambassadors Hotel? They have a fine snack-bar there."

"That'll be swell!" the little boy said eagerly. "We went there once with Granddad. You'll like it, Loris."

"Haven't you been there?" Brett asked her casually.

She turned to look at him, the wind blowing her soft, dark hair about her face. "No. I haven't been out very much since I've been here."

She looked so young and innocent sitting next to him that Brett had a sudden, unaccountable desire to show her all the lovely places he knew so well. The simple white dress she wore made him wish he had the right to buy her expensive, beautiful clothes, and his hands tightened on the steering wheel as he shot the car forward.

Loris was surprised to find that the ground floor of the hotel consisted entirely of an elaborate arcade of shops. And what magnificent shops they were! Exquisite shoes, hats, blouses and flowers were there for the asking – or the buying – and there was a large drug store and an even larger music counter.

Brett led the way along the marble-floored corridor through the rows of shops to a restaurant set with small tables, at one end of which was a long counter with high stools. Without waiting to be asked the children clambered manfully up on them, and Loris found herself sitting next to Brett again while Timothy and Gillian ordered what they wanted.

"What will you have?" Brett asked her. "Shall it be a pineapple sundae like the birthday boy or a double ice-cream soda like Gillian and me?"

"Neither, thank you. I'll just have some coffee."

"Nonsense, have some ice-cream! It'll do you good." His eyes travelled over her figure. "You're thinner, Loris," he added abruptly. "Aren't you well?"

"I'm all right, thank you. It's probably because I'm not used to the heat." She turned away and busied herself with the children, not wishing to say any more, for the sight of Brett's strong, brown hands resting on the counter filled her with so great a longing to be in his arms that she could hardly bear his proximity. 'Oh, Brett,' her heart cried, 'how could you forget so easily? How could you pretend at love when you knew how much every gesture, every word, meant to me? How could you believe I was only playing a game?'

"Loris, I've been talking to you and you haven't been listening to a word," Gillian said plaintively.

Loris forced her attention back to the little girl. "I'm sorry, darling. What is it?"

"I want to know if I can have another sundae."

"I think you've had enough already, dear."

"Well, let me have half, then," the little girl pleaded.

"All right," Loris relented. "But only half. Give the rest of it to Timothy."

"Oh, goody!" Timothy shrilled, his mouth full. "Wish I had a birthday every day. Think of all the food and presents I'd get!"

Brett laughed. "Talking of presents, young man, you haven't been over to collect your puppy. You can come over and take him whenever you like, you know."

"Gee, thanks, Uncle Brett! Can we go tomorrow, Loris?"

"I don't know about tomorrow, dear," she said guardedly, "but we'll go as soon as we can."

Satisfied, the little boy resumed his inroads on the icecream.

"How's Melanie?" Brett asked casually, in an effort to make conversation.

"She's very well," Loris replied briefly. But she wished with all her heart that she could confide in him; tell him all her fears about the girl and how much she disliked the young man with whom Melanie was spending so much of her time. But pride forbade her and she changed the subject by asking him questions about the film studio.

It was with a feeling of relief that she saw the children had finished their ice-cream and, before they could demand anything else, said they must go. Timothy and Gillian clambered down regretfully, casting longing glances at the cream cakes arrayed enticingly along the counter, but about to offer them some, Brett intercepted a glance from Loris and said nothing while she bundled them unceremoniously out of the restaurant.

They drove back in silence, the children replete with food and exhausted by the exertions of the afternoon, while Loris herself was too tired and depressed to make small talk.

It was not until they were nearly home that she spoke to the man by her side. "You needn't drive us to the door. It won't do the children any harm to walk up the drive."

Without demur Brett slowed down and Loris noticed the ease with which he brought the car to a standstill outside the gates. The handle of the car door was stiff and she was struggling to open it when with a murmur of "allow me," he leaned across to do it for her. He was so close that she could see the tiny pulse beating at his temple, while he in turn felt her breath warm against his cheek. But the moment of nearness was soon over and she stepped out of the car and hand in hand with the children stood on the gravel path and watched as he turned the Studebaker round and drove off.

Loris stood motionless until the car had disappeared from sight, then with a heavy heart followed Timothy and Gillian up the drive. They were just approaching the house when a car came up behind them, and as it shot past in a flurry of dust Loris recognized Melanie and Miguel Santos.

By the time they reached the front door Melanie was bidding good-bye to her escort, a slim, dark young man of average height with black, wavy hair and limpid, eloquent brown eyes. In ordinary circumstances Loris could have well understood any girl being flattered by his at-

75

tentions, although she herself viewed him with some distaste, for in contrast to Dickson's wholesome good looks he seemed oily and over-immaculate, with a suaveness suggesting guile.

Miguel gave her a little bow from the waist as she went up the steps. "Good evening, Miss Cameron," he said, with elaborate politeness.

"Good evening." She gave him a cool smile avoiding his glance as she shepherded her charges through the door.

"Wait for me, Loris," Melanie called after her. She extended her hand to Miguel who, with a flash of white teeth placed it against his lips, and Loris heard him murmur: "*Adiós*, beloved. Until tomorrow. . . ."

'Really!' thought Loris with a prickle of annoyance. 'How can Melanie be so stupid as to like that sort of thing?' The lavish compliments Miguel uttered so easily seemed to her so false and cheap that she was surprised at even Melanie being taken in by them, although had she known Melanie's reaction to his approaches earlier that afternoon, she would have been somewhat mollified.

After their bathe they had laid side by side in the sun. Enchanting in a brief white swim suit which emphasized her golden tan and curls bleached to silvery fairness, Melanie looked like a water sprite, and Miguel studied her covertly as she lay beside him, wholeheartedly wishing they were alone so that he could take this elfish creature in his arms and bring her to life with all the ardour and warmth of his Latin temperament.

Driving to a hotel for tea, he had stopped the car in a deserted road and pulled her roughly against him, seeking her mouth with his until his lips were pressed feverishly upon hers. Melanie quivered beneath his experienced touch and responded artlessly to his kiss until his passion began to frighten her and she tried to push him away.

"Don't, Miguel – please don't."

"Melanie, my darling, how much I love you," he

76

breathed, holding her more closely. "You are so fair, so golden and white, that you have taken my heart in your little hands." His own hands gently and insistently stroked her as he spoke. "You are more beautiful than any girl I have ever known, more beautiful and a thousand times more captivating."

Words becoming inadequate, he dropped tiny kisses all over her face, placing the last full upon her mouth until, with a final wrench, she pushed him away again. "No, Miguel, don't."

"But, my darling, you like to kiss me and I like to kiss you, so why shouldn't we make love to each other?"

"Because – because I don't want to." For the first time a picture of Dickson flashed into her mind and she felt ashamed.

Miguel looked down quizzically at her small, set face, and then, with a theatrical sigh, let in the clutch and drove on.

When they had had tea, Melanie found herself nervously wishing she did not have to go home alone with him, but she reckoned without Miguel's shrewdness, for the young man realized he would have to go carefully if he wanted to win this naïve little creature. He was in love with her in so far as he could be in love with anyone, and by nature enjoyed the vicarious pleasure of stealing a girl from another man. Melanie's engagement only increased his interest, but he was too astute not to realize that beneath her impulsiveness she was old-fashioned enough to feel guilty at being kissed by a man other than her fiancé and he took pains to become once more the lighthearted and amusing companion she enjoyed being with.

Melanie breathed a sigh of relief at the change in his behaviour. He was so different from Dickson, who had always been gentleness itself with her and never alarmed her by revealing his passion, that she had been genuinely frightened by the persistence of Miguel's love-making. But the young Argentinian was so natural and

77

inconsequential during the drive home that she felt no apprehension at accepting his invitation to take her out the following day, although had she seen the satisfied smile on his lips as he drove away she might have felt less assured.

CHAPTER VIII

ALTHOUGH she had never looked after children before, Loris settled down quite naturally to the task of taking care of Timothy and Gillian, for she possessed the ability of talking to them in their own language.

Looking after the children gave Loris a peace of mind and contentment that helped her to pass weeks which would otherwise have dragged. With Timothy and Gillian constantly chattering and plying her with questions, and her continuous efforts to keep them amused and happy, she had little time for her own thoughts, and it was only in the evenings, when they were in bed, that her mind was free to think back again to those brief and lovely days on the boat and wonder why an enchantment which had been so complete should have ended so disastrously.

Whenever Brett came to the house she made a point of absenting herself, and except for brief glimpses of him when he called to see Dickson she scarcely saw him at all. Dickson himself never mentioned Brett to her, for he sensed something amiss between them, and he was equally careful to make no mention of Loris when he saw Brett.

Mr. and Mrs. Loftus were kindness itself, and the fact that Loris was now employed by their daughter made no difference in their attitude to her. They often invited her to go with them to a cinema or theatre, but she usually refused, for although she knew that before Elaine had engaged her the children had often been left on their own in the evenings, she did not like to leave them now they were her responsibility. She never bothered to arrange any definite time off, for she had no friends to visit and as she did not look forward to the thought of a long afternoon or evening with nothing to do, did not broach the subject to Elaine, feeling that if an occasion arose when she wanted to go out it would be time enough to ask her then.

After their visit to the film studio the children settled down once more to a regular routine, and for a few days occupied themselves happily with playing film stars and directors, but one morning at breakfast Timothy remembered Brett's promise of the puppy and asked if they could go and fetch it. Although she was dismayed at the prospect of seeing Brett again so soon, Loris realized it would be impossible to try to dissuade the little boy from fetching his dog, and as she had no means of knowing at what time of day she would be least likely to encounter Brett, decided to take the children to his house after lunch on the supposition that he would be working in the afternoon.

Immediately after lunch they set out on foot, and in spite of her apprehensions Loris enjoyed the walk, for there was a slight breeze in the air which made her think nostalgically of a summer's day in England. She wondered what her father would be doing – whether he was working in his study or visiting one of his parishioners, and a wave of homesickness clouded the sunshine.

Brett was in his library when he saw the three figures walking up the drive, and drew back with a muttered exclamation, for he had no desire to meet Loris. Indeed, ever since he had seen her a few days ago, her heart-shaped face with its pensive grey eyes had seldom been out of his mind. Unwillingly now, he was forced to admit that she looked lovely as she moved towards him with that effortless grace which had been one of the first things he had admired about her.

In a white linen dress, with her dark hair falling to her shoulders, she scarcely looked old enough to have charge of Timothy and Gillian, and the two children bouncing happily along on either side of her might have been her small sister and brother instead of members of a different generation. He stood behind the curtain and watched them as they walked around the side of the house, and realized they had come to collect Timothy's puppy.

Loris and the children went straight to the kennels, where Belle and her litter were gambolling happily, and Timothy immediately pounced on the small black spaniel he had marked for his own. He took it up and hugged it against him and Loris, relieved that he had made his choice so quickly, became intent on leaving the grounds before she encountered Brett.

"Come along, Timothy, we'll go into town and buy a lead for him."

"We don't have to go past the house, then, Loris," the little boy replied, "we can follow the path down the garden and through the little wood at the end. That'll lead us to the main road and we can get a bus to Sunset Boulevard."

Loris jumped at the idea of avoiding the house. "Come along, then, you show us the way. But keep a hold on the puppy in case he tries to run back to his mother."

They walked slowly through the gardens and Loris was delighted by the beautifully kept flower beds and spacious lawns. The flowers here were not as simple as the ones that grew in the vicarage garden and she stopped every now and then to examine an unusual bloom, marvelling at the delicate intricacies of a flower or leaf. Presently they came to a small path which led through a copse of evergreens to a clearing, and she was surprised to discover a large, picturesque barn set amongst the trees.

Timothy gave a whoop of delight. "Gee, I wish Granddad had a barn like Uncle Brett. Think of the games we could play in it."

"What do they use it for, Timothy?" Loris asked.

The little boy pondered. "I think it's for parties and barbecues and things."

Timothy was so interested in the barn that he forgot his puppy, and with a wriggle of its small, fat body the little creature freed itself from his grasp and scampered off at high speed in the direction of its mother.

"I'll catch him," Loris called over her shoulder. "You two wait by the barn."

She chased after the puppy, but it was already half-way across the lawn before she caught up with it, and seizing its warm, panting body in her arms, slowly retraced her steps.

Still out of breath, she strolled back along the path to the clearing, then stopped with a gasp of horror. In her absence, Timothy had begun to climb the barn and was already half-way up the roof, while Gillian stood below, anxiously counselling him to come down. The little boy was about fifteen feet above the ground, and Loris caught her breath in fear lest he miss his footing and slip.

Trying to hide the urgency in her voice she called peremptorily to him to come down, but with a war-whoop Timothy continued to climb.

Slowly and laboriously he reached the top and with a gasp of triumph turned to survey the ground. Loris and Gillian seemed a long way away and suddenly his face contracted in terror as he realized the height to which he had climbed.

Loris drew her breath sharply at his expression, and her voice this time was soft and encouraging as she called to him again.

"Come along, Timothy, you've been up there long enough."

With a feeble smile he started to move, but after a moment his hands clutched the roof convulsively and he stopped dead. "I can't, Loris! I can't move! I'm scared. What shall I do?"

Realizing that unless she kept her wits about her he might fall, Loris spoke far more casually than she felt. "There's nothing to be frightened of. It's quite easy. Turn round and go slowly back the way you came."

"I can't, I can't!" the little boy wailed. "The ground's too far away! Oh, I'm so scared!"

Debating whether to run and fetch help, Loris decided it would be unwise to leave him in case he became dizzy and lost his footing. Putting the puppy into Gillian's arms she told her to run to the house and tell someone to bring a ladder. Then she started to climb.

The walls of the barn were rough and it was not difficult to find footholds. As she mounted she talked to Timothy continuously, trying to keep his mind off his fear. "I'm not so good at this as you are, Timothy, but considering I haven't climbed a tree since I was a little girl I'm not doing too badly, am I? Shan't be long now. It's a good job I'm wearing flat shoes or it'd be much more difficult. Nearly there." As she spoke she reached the roof and on her hands and knees began to edge her way towards him.

When she reached him he caught hold of her in such a fierce grip that she staggered and almost toppled them both over.

"Oh, Loris, I'm so glad you came up! I couldn't have climbed down on my own. It's ever so high – you have a look."

She gave him a reassuring pat, but studiously avoided turning round. "There's nothing to be frightened of now, Timothy. You turn round behind me and then we'll both make our way down together. You needn't be scared of slipping because I'll be in front of you."

Trembling, the little boy did as he was told, and very slowly they began to move sideways. In case Timothy should fall against her, Loris gripped the tiles as hard as she could, and by the time they reached the guttering which ran round the eaves her hands were bruised and sore.

They stopped at the guttering, and Loris decided to wait until someone came with a ladder. But Timothy thought otherwise. Now that he was no longer on his own he had regained his self-confidence, and started to clamber down the wall with the agility of a monkey.

Relieved that the worst was over, Loris began to follow him. But suddenly her foot slipped and with a startled cry she fell the remaining ten feet to the ground, landing in a crumpled heap with one leg twisted beneath her.

She lay still for a long moment, the breath shaken out of her body, and before she could recover, felt herself being lifted up in strong arms.

Opening her eyes, she looked into Brett's face. "Are you all right?" he inquired anxiously. "I called out to you to wait for the ladder, but I was too late. I was just in time to see you fall."

"I think I'm all right, thank you." The sight of him aroused her spirit of independence. "Please put me down."

"Don't be silly, I'll carry you up to the house. You've had a nasty fall, you know. You're probably more shaken than you realize."

"Do put me down," she said stubbornly, "I'm sure I can manage."

"As you please, then," he said abruptly, and lowered her to the ground. But the moment her left foot touched the grass a sharp stab of pain shot through her, and if his arm had not still been around her waist she would have fallen.

Without another word, he swung her up into his arms again, and with the two children walking subduedly behind strode through the copse and across the lawn to the house.

Dorcas met them as they came through the door, and Brett sent the old man to fetch bandages and a coldwater compress as he carried Loris into the lounge and put her gently down on to the settee.

Sick with pain, she lay quite inert while Brett gently undid her shoe and examined her ankle. It was swelling rapidly and already turning blue, and with gentle hands he applied the compress and bandaged it on to her foot. Then he left the room, returning after a moment with a glass.

"You'd better drink this. It'll make you feel stronger."

"I'd rather not, thanks – I feel too sick."

"Nonsense, it'll do you good. It's only brandy and water. Take it."

She took the glass and sipped, choking at the first mouthful. But by the time she had finished it the colour was beginning to return to her pallid cheeks and she sat up and smiled at him.

"You've made quite a good job of my ankle."

"All the same, as soon as you get home I'd call a doctor to have a look at it if I were you. Just to make sure nothing's broken."

"The whole thing seems so silly. I should have looked where I was going."

"You can hardly blame yourself for falling," he said abruptly. "I shouldn't think you make a habit of climbing up and down barns."

Loris smiled. "I certainly don't." She moved her foot gingerly and grimaced with pain. "It hurts more than I thought it would," she admitted.

"I suppose you know how lucky you are it wasn't anything more serious?"

Remembering his alarm when Gillian had rushed in for help, Brett suddenly realized how much it would have meant to him if any real harm had come to Loris, and the misunderstandings between them dwindled into insignificance beside his anxiety.

She flushed at the intensity of his tone and looked up at him in surprise. Then, afraid that her own emotion might lead her into reading more into his words than he meant to imply, she tried to bring the conversation on to a more impersonal place.

"This is a charming room, Brett." Her eyes rested appreciatively on the handsome furniture and Persian rugs. There were several fine paintings on the walls which harmonized completely with their surroundings, bespeaking the taste of the collector, and the atmosphere was one of mellow distinction. "Did you have it decorated yourself?" she asked politely.

"Most of the stuff came from my old home in Virginia," he replied. "It's been in the family for some time, so it's lucky for me my forebears seem to have shared my idea of taste! But I don't want to discuss the house now, Loris. There's something much more important to talk about. I want to ask you. . . ."

But at that moment Dorcas came in with the children and their opportunity to talk was lost. Brett looked none too pleased at the interruption and threw a regretful glance at Loris as he turned away.

"Ah'se given the chillun ice-cream and strawberry shortcake in the kitchen," Dorcas explained, "and Massa Timothy's knees has been washed."

"Thank you, Dorcas," Brett said briefly. "Have the car brought round so I can drive Miss Cameron and the children home, will you?" Then to Timothy: "Well, young fella, you deserve a spanking for this afternoon's escapade, and if I didn't think you'd been punished enough by the fright you've had I'd give it to you myself."

He ruffled the boy's tousled head and drew Gillian on to his knee, and within a few minutes the children were at their ease again. The colour came back into their cheeks as the events of the afternoon began to recede, and listening to their laughter and chatter, Loris was touched by Brett's kindness and understanding.

Presently the butler came in again, carrying the puppy in his arms. "Miss Gillian left this little doggy in the kitchen, and the car is heah, Mis' Brett. Ah thought Ah'd bring him in so she don't leave him behind."

"Good." Brett stood up. "Take the children out to the car, Dorcas, and I'll bring Miss Cameron."

The butler shepherded Timothy and Gillian from the room and their voices died away as they went across the hall and out through the front door. Brett moved towards Loris, but she threw her legs over the side of the couch.

"You needn't carry me, you know," she said hastily.

86

"I can manage quite well if you'll give me your arm."

"Do you propose to hop to the door like a kanga-roo?" he asked wryly, and without more ado lifted her and strode out of the room.

Loris put one arm around his neck to balance herself, her heart beating so loudly that she was almost afraid he would hear it. The roughness of his jacket tickled her cheek as she leant against it and she was conscious of his strength and the smell of leather and tweed which emanated from him. He held her as if she weighed no more than a feather, one arm under her knees and the other around her waist, the warmth of his hand pene-trating the thin linen of her dress. She saw a slight flush mount into his cheeks and his jaw muscles clench and unclench. But although he kept his eyes straight ahead, she knew with a little thrill of triumph that he was not as unmoved by her nearness as he appeared to be.

All too soon they reached the car and he put her gently in the back seat, placing her lengthwise on the grey leather upholstery, while Timothy and Gillian clambered into the wide front seat with him.

No one was about when they arrived home, but one of the servants let them into the house, exclaiming in quick concern when she saw Loris's ankle.

Brett carried her straight up the wide staircase and halted at the top. "Which is your room?"

A tremor ran through her and she avoided his eyes. "At the end of the corridor, on the left."

The door was ajar and kicking it open he strode in and deposited her on the bed. "I'll send the maid up to help you," he said abruptly. "Get into bed while I call the doctor."

"Oh, but the children –"

"One of the servants can give them their supper and put them to bed if Elaine isn't home."

"Yes, but –"

"But me no more buts, Loris. Won't you do anything I ask without protesting – or do you just *like* being contrary?" He raised his eyebrows quizzically and she flushed at the gentle mockery in his tone. At that moment there was a knock at the door and Brett swore softly under his breath. "Damn! Will I never get a chance...." As the maid entered he moved away from the bed. "I'll go on back home when I've called the doctor. You look as though you need a good night's rest. I'd like to come over tomorrow, though. I shall be at the office all day – there's some darned conference – but I should be free by about five-thirty, if that'll be O.K.?" Loris nodded speechlessly. "Good. See you tomorrow." Then to the maid: "See that Miss Cameron doesn't get up, will you? I don't trust her to obey *me*!" With a swift smile that included them both he went out, leaving a puzzled and wildly hoping Loris.

Mr. and Mrs. Loftus were most concerned when they heard what had happened and congratulated Loris on her resourcefulness in rescuing their errant grandson, and even Elaine went out of her way to be nice when she went in to see her later that evening. She roamed round the room, dropping ash on the carpet and restlessly touching the curtains and the ornaments on the dressing-table as she talked.

"It was grand of you, Loris – thanks a lot. I hope the little devil's learnt his lesson, although I doubt if anything will stop him getting into mischief."

"I'm sure he didn't mean any harm, Mrs. Forrest. Boys are naturally adventurous and you can't put a curb on them all the time. He's very well behaved on the whole."

"He certainly seems to show you his best side. He's a limb of Satan when I have to look after him."

"Well, I hope you won't have to for very long – I should be all right again in a few days."

"Don't worry about that," Elaine said abruptly. "I don't mind looking after them once in a while. It makes a change and Gillian's rather sweet." She gave a stifled yawn. "Well, I must be on my way. I've got a party tomorrow and I don't want to look too much of a wreck for it." She sauntered to the door and with a wave of her hand went out.

Loris lay back on the pillows, wishing half enviously, half wistfully, that she was as sophisticated and soignée as her employer. She could not understand how any man could fail to find Elaine attractive, and wondered why, if all the woman had said were true, Brett had not married her long ago. It could not have been lack of opportunity.

Strange how her thoughts revolved around one man. No matter what she started to think about, she always ended up thinking of Brett. Loris smiled to herself as she remembered how annoyed he had been at Dorcas's interruption that afternoon. What was it he had been trying to say? Did he want to explain his silence in New York? – his coldness to her since his return to California? The obvious change in his attitude to her on the boat? There was a lot of explaining to be done before they could get back on the old footing again. And yet would it ever be the old footing? She was not the same girl he had known on the boat. Her weeks in California had shown her another world, another way of life, and although she was still fundamentally the same unaffected young woman, experience had taught her to be less spontaneous and trusting, and she knew that when she met Brett tomorrow evening, she would meet him more as an equal than ever before.

CHAPTER IX

DURING the night the bandage with which the doctor had bound Loris's ankle made it throb painfully, and when Dickson's nurse redressed it in the morning it was so stiff and discoloured that she was not allowed to get up.

The bedroom windows were thrown wide open and the sunshine streamed in, touching the cream walls with fingers of light. Dickson sent up some books and magazines, but she could not be bothered to concentrate on even the lightest reading – for the adventures of the day before had told on her – and she was content to doze intermittently until lunch was sent up on a tray.

Melanie popped in for a little while, but seeing how tired Loris was, did not stay long, and promised to come and sit with her during the afternoon instead.

After their quarrel in the lounge, the subject of Miguel had not been broached between them again, and had it not been for her disquiet at leaving Melanie, Loris would have returned to England there and then, for she had been deeply hurt by the girl's remark. But next day Melanie had apologized for losing her temper, and her childishness had had such an endearing quality that Loris could not help forgiving her.

She knew that at heart Melanie was anything but worthless. It was only her youth and the spoiling which over-indulgent parents had given her that made her selfishly wilful and thoughtless. Given time, the pursuit of pleasure she was now so feverishly engaged in would burn itself out, and Loris felt sure she would eventually settle down to a happily married life.

If anyone had asked Melanie whether she was in love with Dickson she would have answered "Yes", without any hesitation, for even though she found Miguel and his friends exciting and gay, Dickson still held first place in her heart, and in spite of her 'don't care' attitude she was troubled by their estrangement no less than the rift between herself and Loris. If she sensed her friend's instinctive dislike and mistrust of Miguel she pretended to be unconcerned by it, and sometimes regarded Loris's calm face with annoyance, remembering the old carefree days when the atmosphere between them had been warm and affectionate. But although she shrugged her shoulders and pretended to be indifferent, she longed to be able to confide in Loris as she had done in the old days, and the accident gave her the opportunity she had been seeking.

Immediately after lunch she ran upstairs, hoping that the long rest in bed had proved sufficient and that Loris would now be in the mood for some company.

This was the first occasion they had really been alone together since their quarrel, and Melanie took Loris's hand and squeezed it impulsively as it lay on the coverlet, fervently hoping her friend would accept the olive branch she was offering.

But the sight of Loris's pale face proved too much for her, and her carefully prepared speech was forgotten as she burst out:

"Loris, what's the matter between us?"

"The matter? Nothing, why do you ask?" Loris answered casually, trying not to show how pleased she was that Melanie's mask of indifference was beginning to crack.

"But there *is* something wrong." Melanie sat down and swung one leg backwards and forwards as it dangled over the edge of the bed. "Things haven't been the same ever since – ever since I –"

"Ever since you were annoyed because I said I didn't approve of your attitude towards Dickson?" Loris prompted gently.

Melanie had the grace to flush. "I did flare up, didn't I? It must have been because I realized I was in the wrong." There was a pause. "But I want you to understand the way I feel about Dickson. It isn't that I don't love him – I do. It's just that if I'm with him the whole time, we always seem to end up biting each other's heads off. I don't blame him – I'm just as much at fault myself. But it isn't only me, Loris – you do believe that, don't you?"

"Of course I do. It isn't easy for either of you. But it's only because Dickson loves you so much that he gets upset. That's why you should be patient with him."

"I try to be, honestly I do, but it's hard to keep cheerful and smiling when you feel you want to scream! The only way I can go on is by getting a change of atmosphere." Then, in a small voice: "Loris, have you ever thought about my future – what will become of me if Dickson doesn't get well? Do you think we'd be able to make our marriage work with him always in his present condition?" She fingered the bedspread nervously. "I'm not kidding myself, Loris – I know I'm young and spoilt and that I've never had to face up to things, but if I don't understand anyone else, I do at least understand myself, and you know as well as I do that I wouldn't make an ideal wife for Dickson if he didn't get better."

"No one could be expected to make an ideal wife under those conditions, Melanie. But I don't think Dickson is looking for an ideal wife. I can't tell whether or not you'd be happy with him if you were married, but I don't think he'd expect you to marry him unless he got better."

"I've thought about that as well," Melanie replied slowly. "I know he loves me, and it would be a great sacrifice to give me up. But do you think I'd be right to accept such a sacrifice even if he made it? How do you think I'd feel if I agreed to do it and took the easy way out?"

Loris was surprised that Melanie had given so much thought to her problem. "I can't answer that for you, my dear. It's something you'll have to work out for yourself."

"But what would you do if it happened to you? If it were –"

She stopped, and Loris realized she had been about to mention Brett's name. If Melanie had been surprised that what had seemed the beginning of a lasting love had petered out so dismally, she had been tactful enough never to speak of it.

"If it had happened to – to the man I love, then I – well, it wouldn't make any difference," Loris said quietly. "But that's nothing to go by, darling, because no two people are alike. What I'd find easy, you might find difficult, and there are lots of things you could do which I'd never even attempt. If Dickson doesn't get better, I'd be the last person in the world to urge you to marry him if you didn't want to. It would be far better to tell him before, than marry him and make him even more unhappy afterwards." She took Melanie's hand. "But why talk about such morbid things? There's no point in crossing your bridges until you come to them, and at the moment we can still hope he'll be all right."

"But there doesn't seem to *be* much hope, Loris. Some of the best specialists in America have seen him, and they can't even find out what's the matter. Martin Abel saw him the other day, and even *he* was in the dark."

They both fell silent, Melanie remembering the eminent nerve specialist's remarks to Dickson's family after he had come from examining him. His face had been kindly and non-committal as he had explained to them that as far as he could tell there was nothing to stop the patient from walking again.

"There's no damage to the nerve tissues, and it's my belief that his paralysis is the result of shock. There is a form of shock treatment we could try, but it often has violent effects – the patient might go into convulsions while under treatment, or the shock of the electric impulses might cause a broken arm or strained muscle." He paused, then went on: "Today, however, we administer the minutest dose of curare, which, as you may know, is a poison the Indians used to put on the tips of their spears. It's very deadly and only the smallest amount can be injected, but it helps the patient to relax so that the shock he receives has a less drastic effect. We could try it, of course, but it's usually only used where there is known to be a mental anxiety, and personally I wouldn't advise it in this case. I think if a shock *were* to do the trick, the patient must be conscious when it occurs, and this form of treatment makes that impossible. My advice is to wait a little longer and then, if nothing happens – perhaps you'll get another opinion."

"But we understand you are the foremost authority on cases of this kind," Edward Loftus said, his face strained.

Mr. Abel inclined his head in acknowledgment, and Mrs. Loftus interposed: "Are you suggesting that if my son received a severe shock, he might recover?"

"That might be the case," the specialist conceded, "but of course, by shock I don't mean somebody making a sudden noise or throwing cold water over him. It would have to be a shock sufficient to impel the nervous system to react in a violent manner."

"And if he never gets such a shock?"

"Then I cannot say what will happen."

Loris watched the changes of expression flit across Melanie's face, mirroring her unhappy thoughts, and was filled with sympathy for her.

"Try not to worry too much about it," she said gently. "I'm sure things will work out all right in the end."

Melanie sighed. "I wonder. Sometimes I think it would have been better if Dickson and I had never met." Then, with a lightning change of mood: "I must go and get dressed now. Mr. and Mrs. Loftus are taking me to the opening of the Golden Slipper Club, so I mustn't be late." She bent and kissed Loris and then stood up. "I'm glad you didn't go back, darling. Although I haven't seen much of you lately, just knowing you're here and I can talk to you has made all the difference."

"Always come to me if there's anything you think I can do, darling. I'll try to understand."

"Oh, Loris, you sound so grown-up and worldly-wise that you make me feel like a baby." With a sigh she went into her own bedroom and shut the door.

Loris did not wish to be in bed when Brett called to see her and although she found it extremely difficult to dress herself, decided to manage as best she could. But it was a slow and tedious process and Melanie and the Loftuses had already left the house before she was ready. Negotiating the stairs was even worse, and she had to restrain a desire to sit down and shuffle from step to step, afraid that Brett might walk in and discover her making this indecorous descent. It took some time before she gained the hall and when she reached the lounge door she was longing to sit down and rest her feet.

She turned the knob and then halted in consternation. Dickson was lying on the couch, propped up by cushions, his head buried in his hands in an attitude of abject misery.

Loris hobbled over to him as quickly as she could, and did not speak until she was kneeling by his side.

"What is it, Dickson? What's the matter?"

The boy raised a ravaged face. "I guess I've reached the end of my tether, Loris. I can't go on like this any longer. I've tried to be cheerful, hoping I might suddenly wake up and find it's all a bad dream, but there doesn't seem to be any future for me."

"Don't say that, Dickson. You've got Melanie. *She's* your future."

He laughed shortly. "I haven't got her, Loris, and you needn't pretend otherwise. You don't have to be kind when you know as well as I do that I've lost her."

"But you haven't! Melanie loves you. Only this afternoon she told me so. She...."

"Don't string me along," he broke in bitterly. "I wouldn't expect her to marry me as I am now, and the longer we go on together like this, the worse things will

95

get. Even if she still wanted to marry me we wouldn't stand a chance of happiness. No, my only hope is to send her away and try to make a life without her, although God knows how I'll bring myself to do it." He covered his face again and his body was racked with sobs.

It was the first time in her life Loris had seen a man cry and she was more moved than she would have believed possible. Filled with an overwhelming desire to comfort him she drew his head on to her shoulder, stroking his fair hair and murmuring soft, incoherent words of sympathy.

Slowly his weeping subsided, but his head remained on her shoulder, as if he drew comfort from her gentleness and calm. Loris did not move for a long while, afraid of disturbing him, and was so engrossed that she failed to hear the door open, or see Brett standing there looking down at them.

Brett saw her hand moving over the fair head again and again and listened to her soft murmurings. Then, hardly conscious of what he was doing, he closed the door softly behind him and stood with his back to it, trying to regain his self-control.

When they had been together the day before, he had sensed Loris's eagerness to see him alone this evening and would have staked everything he possessed that she was as anxious as he to clear up the misunderstanding between them. To discover her now with Dickson in her arms was so incredible that if he had not seen it with his own eyes he would never have believed it.

With heavy tread he walked through the hall and had just reached the front door when he heard his name called. He looked up dazedly and saw Elaine coming down the stairs, dressed for the evening.

"Why, Brett, what are you doing here?"

He did not answer, and as she came nearer she was shocked at the greyness of his face and his distraught expression. Putting a hand on his arm, she drew him into

96

the library, went to the sideboard and without speaking poured him a stiff whisky and soda.

He drank it at a gulp, then set the glass down and made as if to go.

"No, Brett, don't leave yet. You haven't got a date, have you?"

"No," he said dully.

If Elaine was surprised at his manner – for he was acting like an automaton – she made no comment. "Got a cigarette for me?"

Without a word he offered his case. "Thanks." She took one, lit it and blew a cloud of smoke into the air. "I'm going to a party tonight," she went on casually. "If you're not doing anything, how about taking me somewhere for dinner and then coming along to it with me afterwards?"

He poured himself a liberal glass of whisky and took a gulp. "I'm certainly in the mood for gaiety!" he said bitterly. "But what the hell? O.K., Elaine, I'll stake you to a dinner – *and* go to your party with you."

He strode out of the room and by the time Elaine had fetched her wrap was sitting at the wheel of his car, staring straight ahead of him. She got in with a thrill of elation at the thought of the evening ahead, and put one hand affectionately beneath his unyielding arm.

Loris heard the sound of a car and jerked her head up, but the noise faded into the distance and she thought with a pang of disappointment that it could not be Brett arriving.

Dickson moved his head and looked up at her sheepishly. "I'm sorry I've made such a fool of myself, Loris."

"You've nothing to apologize for, Dickson. Anyone might have done the same." She stood up and hobbled over to a chair.

"Gee, I'm a selfish brute! I forgot to ask you how you're feeling after your accident."

She smiled. "Oh, I'm all right. In fact, I'm so much

97

better that I feel a bit of a fraud limping around like this."

There was a knock at the door and she gave a nervous start, but it was only the maid to announce that dinner was ready and to inquire whether Miss Cameron would have it in the dining-room or with Mr. Dickson.

"I'll have it with you, Dickson, shall I?"

"I'd be mortally offended if you didn't."

They chatted without embarrassment over their trays, although Loris jumped so obviously at every sound that Dickson asked if she was expecting anyone. She was saved from having to answer his question by the advent of the maid bringing in the sweet, and did her best after that to conceal her feelings. But by nine o'clock her anxiety was difficult to hide and she pictured Brett lying ill or having been involved in an accident, and was full of fear lest Melanie's question might find an answer in her own life. She was thankful when the nurse appeared and wheeled Dickson away to bed, for the effort of maintaining conversation was beginning to tell on her, and after he had gone she sat on alone in the lounge, unable to concentrate either on her book or her sewing.

Then with a faint sigh her thoughts reverted to Brett and why he had not called until, lulled by the warmth of the fire and the comfort of her chair, she fell asleep.

Awakened by the slamming of a car door, Loris sat up with a start and glanced at her watch, surprised to see it was nearly one o'clock. Painfully she got to her feet and reached the door just as Elaine let herself into the house.

"Hallo, Loris, you still up?" she asked indifferently.

"I fell asleep in front of the fire," Loris explained.

"Oh." A speculative gleam came into Elaine's green eyes. "I thought maybe you'd been stood up on a date or something. You look about as tired as I feel." She slipped off her wrap and stood there yawning, vivid in a sheath-like gown of emerald green, her hair gleaming like copper beneath the light.

98

"Did you have a nice time?" Loris inquired, more out of politeness than interest.

"Swell, thanks, although Brett was so tight, poor pet, I didn't dare let him drive home himself. I dropped him off at his house and came home in his car. He'll have to send someone to fetch it in the morning."

She chatted on gaily, but Loris was not listening, for her brain seemed powerless to absorb anything except the fact that Brett had spent the evening with Elaine.

"Lord, I'm tired," Elaine stretched gracefully. "I'm going to bed and from the look of you that's where you should be, too." With a wave of her hand she walked upstairs and Loris went mechanically into the lounge to collect her book.

She hobbled slowly up the stairs to her room and undressed in a state of torpor. Only when she was lying between the sheets did she give way to the misery and hurt, of contempt not only for Brett but for herself for still loving him, in spite of what she knew him to be.

CHAPTER X

WHEN Brett opened his eyes the following morning, sunshine was already flooding the room. He turned his head to look at the clock and a sharp stab of pain made him wince and put his hand to his temples. With a groan he sat up, then slowly and carefully reaching for the bell he rang for Dorcas, and when the butler appeared, ordered coffee – "as black and strong as you can make it."

After Dorcas had gone he lay still, trying to recollect what had happened the night before. But he could only remember discovering Loris and Dickson in each other's arms, and then driving off in his car with Elaine. Where they had eaten, and to whose party they had gone afterwards, remained a mystery, but he must obviously have drunk more than was good for him, for how he had got home or who had put him to bed he did not know.

The butler came in with coffee and poured it out, and Brett sat up carefully and took the cup. "How did I get home last night, Dorcas?"

"Mrs. Forest brought you back, suh. She took yo' car and drove herself home in it."

Brett swore softly. "Lord, I must have been drunk!"

"Can ah get you anything else, suh?" the old man asked impassively.

"Yes, you can bring me an Alka-Seltzer."

"Ah'm sorry, Mis' Brett, ah plum forgot to bring one along with the coffee."

"That's all right, Dorcas – I'm not in the habit of having hangovers, so I guess you didn't think."

As soon as Dorcas went out Brett reached for the telephone and dialled the Loftus number. A second or two later he was put through to Elaine and her voice, light and sibilant, came over the line.

"How are you this morning, Elaine?"

"I'm fine, Brett. But how are you? You should have a terrible hangover right now."

He gave a short laugh. "I have. Thanks for driving me home. Hope I didn't disgrace myself last night, but I can't remember a darned thing."

There was a short silence and he would have been puzzled if he had seen Elaine's expression. She had only just awakened before Brett telephoned and had lain in bed thinking over the events of the previous night. The implication of Loris's drawn face and the fact that she had stayed up so late for no apparent reason had not been lost on her, and she was willing to bet that Brett's distraught manner had some connection with the girl. Brett had been extremely drunk last night – a rare occurrence where he was concerned – but that he had no recollection of anything that had happened during the evening put an idea into her mind which seemed to become more feasible the longer she thought about it.

"Are you still there, Elaine?"

Infusing the appropriate emotion into her voice, Elaine answered softly: "Don't you remember anything about last night, Brett? Don't you even remember...." She seemed to hesitate, and he prompted:

"Is there anything special I *ought* to remember?"

Her voice trembled effectively. "Unless you don't consider asking me to marry you something special?"

Brett stared at the telephone incredulously, at a loss for words, and it was Elaine's turn to ask: "Are *you* still there? You do remember, don't you, Brett? We were alone in the garden at Mimi Fawsett's place and you were so sweet that – that I –"

Her unaccustomed diffidence touched him. "Why, of course I remember, Elaine." But although he spoke kindly, his face was blankly incredulous as he uttered the words.

"Darling, I'm so glad! I couldn't have borne it if you'd regretted asking me. I've waited so long! Oh, Brett, hurry up and come over, I'm longing to see you.

I must go now, my bath's running, but please don't be long. Au revoir, darling."

Brett replaced the receiver and lay staring at the sun-washed wall at the foot of his bed, cursing himself for a drunken fool. Why hadn't he realized that in the state of mind he was in last night he might do something he would regret? Why hadn't he come home to drink, if drink he must? Why had he ever accepted Elaine's invitation? Why? Why? Why? The fruitless questions hammered in his brain.

He contemplated the idea of going over to see Elaine immediately, and making a clean breast of everything, but he shrank from hurting her, especially as by this time she had probably told her parents, as well as Dickson and – Loris.

Loris! What would her reaction be when she heard about it? Dismissing the bitter hope that she would be as hurt as he had been hurt last night, he wondered whether her vanity would be wounded that he had consoled himself so quickly with someone else. Had she waited for him and wondered why he had not turned up, or had she been so engrossed with Dickson that she had not even noticed or cared that he had not kept his promise? With a groan he got out of bed – if he needed a reason for going on with this farce of an engagement, the idea of hurting Loris would be reason enough in itself.

Elaine felt no compunction at the lie she had told Brett, and his reception of it only filled her with triumph. Ever since they had met she had been determined to marry him, and the fact that she was going to achieve her ambition by means of a lie in no way detracted from her satisfaction.

She, too, wondered what Loris would say when she heard of the engagement, but no remorse stirred her at the thought of having come between two people who, until she had manoeuvred them apart, had obviously been in love with each other. She bathed and dressed

102

quickly, and went downstairs to find her parents so that she could tell them the news before Brett's arrival.

Mr. and Mrs. Loftus were delighted. They had always looked on Brett with affection, and when he arrived, he was immediately shown into the lounge where they greeted him warmly.

"I'm so happy," Mabel Loftus said, kissing him heartily. "I've known for a long time Elaine was in love with you, and it's wonderful to know you feel the same way."

Although he met their congratulations with a polite smile, Brett realized that to ask Elaine to release him was going to be even more difficult than he had imagined.

At that moment there was a sound of children's voices and Timothy and Gillian rushed into the room, slowly followed by Loris, who was walking painfully with the aid of a stick.

"I didn't know you were taking the children over again today, Loris," Elaine said, with unwonted sweetness. "Are you feeling well enough?"

"Yes, thank you, Mrs. Forrest," Loris replied politely, although she did not add that it was only the thought of another long day without anything to do which had made her resume her duties.

"I was going to take them down to the beach," Elaine continued, "but as things have turned out perhaps it's just as well you're in charge again."

Mrs. Loftus saw Loris's puzzled expression and hastened to explain. "You haven't heard my daughter's good news, Loris – she and Brett are going to be married."

In that instant Loris was glad her sleepless night had already given her a pallor, for otherwise the wave of faintness which swept over her would have been noticeable. She clutched the back of a nearby chair to steady herself, and forced a smile to her lips as she turned to Elaine, studiously avoiding Brett's eyes.

"Congratulations, Mrs. Forrest. I hope you'll both be very happy." Then with a little gesture she motioned the children to follow and left the room.

If Brett had expected to gain any satisfaction from Loris's reaction to the news, he was disconcerted to find that far from amusing him, the sight of her white face filled him with distress, and it was only by keeping a firm grip on himself that he refrained from going after her.

But even Mrs. Loftus had noticed Loris's expression, and she remarked on it. "I must say the poor child seemed rather taken aback at the news. For a moment I thought she was going to cry."

Mr. Loftus lit a cigar. "She was probably thinking of Melanie. After all, if it hadn't been for Dickson's accident, it would be her little friend who was getting married."

"Possibly," his daughter murmured ambiguously.

After that, conversation became general, and Brett was thwarted in all his attempts to be alone with Elaine and tell her that the engagement was a mistake, for Mrs. Loftus remained with them all the morning, discussing plans for the wedding.

"There's nothing to stop you getting married as soon as you like," she said happily. "So why not have the wedding before the children go to school?"

"We haven't got as far as making plans yet, Mother — after all we're only just engaged," Elaine protested, although to herself she admitted the wisdom of marrying as soon as possible, doubting whether, once he had had time to think about it, Brett would go through with their marriage.

She glanced down at her watch. "Darn! I've got an appointment with the dressmaker at twelve. I think I'll call her up and put it off. I'm too excited to stand still long enough to be pinned!" She flashed Brett a smile. He looked so maddeningly inaccessible that she longed to be in his arms and make him quicken with desire for her, confident in the knowledge that he would not be human if he failed to respond to her own urgent longing.

"I'll come along with you, Elaine," Mrs. Loftus interposed. "If you're calling Thérèse I'll have a word with her at the same time."

Mother and daughter left the room together, and Brett stood up and paced agitatedly backwards and forwards, running nervous fingers through his dark hair. With every passing moment the situation was becoming more and more difficult, and the longer it was allowed to go on the more impossible it would be to extricate himself.

The sound of children's voices drew him out on to the terrace, and he saw Timothy and Gillian playing on the lawn while Loris sat near them, her ankle resting on a stool.

When she had left the lounge her only desire had been to hide, but the children had made it impossible for her to be alone, and she had taken them out into the garden, resolutely controlling her tears.

During a sleepless night she had made up her mind to see Brett and ask him what it was he had intended saying to her last night and why he had not come. It was ridiculous for two intelligent people to go on misunderstanding each other and she would tell him without false pride that she had waited for him all the evening and ask him what had prevented him from keeping his promise.

Now there was no need, for the answer was quite plain. She doubted that he was really in love with Elaine and wondered dully whether he had asked her to marry him to prove to himself that she, Loris, no longer meant anything to him. The widening stream of misunderstanding seemed to bear her away on a flood of misery, and she knew that they were further apart now than they had ever been.

She shifted her ankle gently and tilted the canopy above her deck chair to shade her from the glare of the sun. The heat was so intense that it seemed to throb around her and the lawn and flower-beds shimmered in a haze.

From the terrace Brett stood watching her, and then,

almost without thinking, walked down the steps and crossed the lawn.

"Loris, I. . . ." He stopped, for he had no idea what he wanted to say. A pang of anguish shot through him at the sight of the pain in her eyes, and he wanted to gather her into his arms and kiss it away. Ironically, he realized his own folly, because he had committed himself to one woman when his whole being cried out for another, and she because of her love for the man who was engaged to her best friend. How much simpler life would have been if he had not come in upon that scene in the lounge last night! He might have been engaged to Loris this morning, instead of to Elaine, and he wished with all his heart that it was so. Then at least one of them would have been happy, for he knew that just to be with her would be happiness enough for him.

Scarcely conscious of what she was saying, Loris took up the conversation where he had left it in mid-air, intent only on breaking a silence which was becoming unbearable.

"My ankle's much better this morning – I can walk quite well today, whereas yesterday I could only hobble."

"I'm glad. You came downstairs yesterday evening for the first time, didn't you?"

"Yes. Melanie went out with Mr. and Mrs. Loftus, and Dickson and I spent the evening together."

"I know you did. I nearly intruded on your privacy."

She was startled at the harshness of his voice, and replied sharply: "Then I'm glad you didn't. Elaine would have been furious if you'd kept her waiting."

"I had no arrangement to go out with Elaine last night until I saw you and Dickson together."

Loris's voice trembled. "What are you trying to imply?"

"I'm not implying anything, I'm merely stating a fact." His anger was rising. "I'd advise you not to trespass on other people's property."

"When I want your advice I'll ask for it. Up to now, I've managed quite well without it."

"I'm sure you have. But if I were you I'd leave Dickson alone. Or have you no qualms about stealing your best friend's fiancé?"

Suddenly, with startling clarity, Loris realized what he meant, and knew he must have come into the lounge as she was comforting Dickson. Seeing them so close together he had misinterpreted their proximity as an embrace! A scarlet flush of indignation mounted to her cheeks, but Brett read it as a sign of guilt.

"You must have a very low opinion of me to say a thing like that." Her voice trembled as she struggled to control her anger.

"I base my opinions on the evidence of my eyes," he returned icily.

"Then you must be blind."

"I certainly have been. But I'm not any more."

"How dare you!" Loris retorted angrily. "As you seem to think so little of me I'd be glad if you'd leave me alone and go back to your fiancée. We have nothing more to say to each other."

Furiously Brett turned on his heel and strode away.

He reached the lounge just as Elaine and her mother returned, and Mrs. Loftus came straight towards him.

"Edward and I want to give a party to celebrate your engagement, Brett," she announced gaily.

For an instant Brett hesitated, undecided whether or not to stop this thing before it had gone any further. But almost as the thought occurred to him his anger at Loris flared up again and he realized the pointlessness of regaining his freedom. Freedom for what? To go on living the loveless life he had endured for so long? Wasn't it better to take whatever love was offered and fill his life, if not with the substance of his desire, at least with its shadow?

"It's very kind of you," he said stiffly, "but I intended holding a party myself in any case – for Melanie and

Dickson – so how about letting me give it as I'd planned and making it out engagement party as well?"

Elaine drew her arm through his and leant against him. "If you're always so considerate, darling, I can see I'm going to be very happy."

He smiled at her briefly. "That's settled then. I'll see about getting the barn fixed up for dancing and we can have a barbecue supper on the lawn."

Mrs. Loftus sighed happily. "Most men never seem to know what kind of party to give. My husband usually leaves it all to me and doesn't care whether it's a picnic or a formal dinner. Thank goodness you know exactly what you want, so all we have to decide on now is who to ask."

"How about giving me a list of the people you'd like to have, and I can add my own friends to it?"

"Elaine can do that for me, Brett. I've got to go and speak to Cook about lunch."

Mrs. Loftus bustled out and for the first time since his arrival at the house Brett was alone with Elaine.

She moved close to him, her hair brushing against his cheek. "You've made me the happiest woman in the world, Brett – or have I said that before?"

Almost against his will he was aware of her heavy intoxicating perfume.

"Elaine, I –"

"Don't say anything to spoil it, darling. Just hold me in your arms." Her voice was languorous. "When you asked me to marry you last night you were so sweet – and humble, too, quite unlike your usual self!" Her imagination started to run away with her. "I'll never forget the wonderful things you said or the way you kissed me."

"I'm sorry if I –"

She silenced him by putting her fingertips over his mouth. "There's no need to be sorry, darling. If you kiss me now like you did then," she whispered, "you'll make me even happier."

Her arms stole up around his neck and he pulled her

towards him, seeing in his mind's eye Loris's flushed, guilty face, and with a little groan he sought Elaine's mouth with his own, trying to find forgetfulness in her passionate response. After a moment she drew back with a satisfied sigh and moved over to the mirror, patting her hair complacently as she did so.

Brett lit a cigarette with a hand that shook, thinking that if he wanted to forget Loris, Elaine might after all prove a means of doing so. Although he had never realized before how responsive she could be, he felt bleakly that if passion alone could suffice he might at least find solace in her arms.

"Penny for your thoughts, Brett." Their eyes met in the mirror, and throwing away his cigarette he reached out and pulled her roughly towards him again.

"They're not worth a cent," he said thickly, and his mouth came down on hers, hard and demanding, stifling her half-hearted protestations.

In the days that followed Brett was a frequent visitor to the house, for there were a hundred and one details to be settled for the coming party. Melanie received the news of the engagement with mixed feelings, for she had thought Brett was in love with Loris. But when she mentioned the subject Loris's reply was so laconic that she was forced to the conclusion that whatever had happened between Brett and Loris on the boat had meant very little to either of them.

Loris was thankful that the days were fine so that she could keep the children out most of the time and thus avoid seeing Brett. Whenever Timothy knew Brett was coming he would want to be there and Loris became quite adept at getting him out of the house and down to the beach instead. As far as Loris could see, the only good thing about Brett's forthcoming marriage to Elaine was the fact that in Brett the children would have a very good stepfather, and they themselves viewed the prospect with delight, anticipating the pleasure of having an understanding father of their own like their other young friends, and last but by no means least, being able to play in the barn as often as they liked!

Meanwhile preparations for the engagement party went ahead. Although it was being held at Brett's house Elaine still had a lot to do and she saw to it that everyone helped her, with the exception of Loris whom she left strictly alone. But Loris would not have been human if she had not found the constant excitement and antici- pation a painful reminder of what it portended, and looked forward to the day when Elaine would leave the house altogether, even though she knew it would be as Brett's wife. Better that than to have to see the beautiful face with its provocative expression and hear the insolent voice continually saying Brett's name; better to know that Brett and Elaine were married and the door on the might-have-been was closed once and for all, than to dream dreams that would never come true.

Loris's first instinct when she received her invitation was to refuse it. But the party had been fixed to coincide with Melanie's twenty-first birthday, and rather than hurt her, Loris braced herself to go through the ordeal of watching other people toasting Brett and Elaine's hap- piness. It was only loyalty to Melanie that had stopped her from returning to England immediately.

But if at times her homesickness and unhappiness about Brett threatened to overwhelm her, Loris was de- termined to look her best at his party and decided to go to one of the many lovely stores in Hollywood or Los Angeles for her dress. However, Mrs. Loftus gave her the name of her own *couturière* and assured her the woman would make her a far better dress than she could buy ready-made, and not wishing to appear ungracious Loris went to Madame Thérèse.

"You leave it to her," Mabel Loftus urged. "Once she's seen you she'll know the exact style to make. But I'd better warn you not to argue with her! She's a French- woman with a very artistic temperament and nothing annoys her more than being told what to do."

110

Nevertheless, although she left the styling of the dress entirely in the Frenchwoman's capable hands, Loris insisted on the colour being black, hoping she would then be able to wear it in England.

Returning from a fitting at the dress salon late one afternoon a few days before the party, Loris went up to her room to find Melanie pinning her hair before having a bath.

"You've been a long time," she remarked as Loris came into the room. "Is your dress nearly ready?"

"Just about. But if I have another prick from a pin I'll tell her to keep it! Next time I want a new dress I'm having one off the peg," Loris said ruefully.

"Nonsense," Melanie grinned. "If you want to be smart you must pay the price."

"I don't know that I want to be all *that* smart."

"Well, if you're going to follow in the footsteps of the stars you'll have to wear something different every day – and at least three wedding dresses!"

"What, for the same man!"

Melanie laughed. "That's your vicarage upbringing coming out again, darling! Of course not for the same man – three different ones!"

"I'm not sure I want to get married at all, let alone three times." Loris took off her coat and hung it in the wardrobe, her voice muffled against the clothes.

"Every girl wants to get married," Melanie said complacently, "and you'll want to marry someone one day as well." She leant against the dressing-table, her expression reflective. "Loris, do you remember the talk we had about Dickson and me a few weeks ago?" She paused and Loris nodded. "Well, I've decided not to see Miguel or any of Dickson's friends any more – unless I'm with him, of course – because that's how it'd be if I were married to Dickson, and I want these next few weeks to be a sort of trial."

Loris's face lit up. "Oh, Melanie, I'm glad you're going to give it a chance! I'm sure that if you and Dickson are

111

together more often you'll understand each other better and won't want to be with him again, to hear his voice and touch him and –" Suddenly she could not go on and turned away, groping for a handkerchief.

It was the first time Melanie had seen Loris cry and she stared at her in consternation. "Loris darling, whatever's the matter?"

"N – nothing. I'll be all right in a minute. It's probably nerves."

"It's more than nerves," Melanie said firmly. "Come on, out with it. I know there's something wrong and I'm not leaving you alone till you tell me what it is."

It was as if Melanie's words broke the dam of Loris's self-control, and the tears rained down her cheeks as she gave herself up to the blessed relief of crying – crying for all the past unhappy weeks and for a future which, as far as she could see, would be a lonely, empty one.

With an exclamation Melanie drew her to the bed and sat with her arms around her until at last the sobbing ceased and there was silence.

"Is it Brett?" Melanie asked gently. Tears welled up in Loris's eyes again and she turned her head away. "But, darling, I never dreamed you still cared. I thought it was just an infatuation that petered out when you both left the ship."

"For him, perhaps, but not for me."

"Oh, Loris, I'm so sorry! How terrible to have to see him with Elaine. It's bad enough now, but before, when you were working for her, it must have been awful." A thought struck her. "You only stayed because of me, didn't you? If things had been right between Dickson and me you'd have gone home long ago and might have forgotten Brett by now." She stood up in distress. "The whole thing's my fault!"

"Of course it isn't," Loris interposed. "It wouldn't have made any difference when I went. The minute I met him it was too late for me to run away."

"Do you still love him so much, then?" Loris nodded,

not trusting herself to speak, and quick tears of sympathy welled up in Melanie's eyes. "Is there anything I can do? I mean, if you'd rather not go to the party we could think up some excuse – pretend I'm ill and that you had to stay with me."

In spite of herself Loris laughed. "Don't be silly, darling. I wouldn't dream of spoiling your party."

"But it's Brett's engagement too and they're sure to make a hullabaloo of it. Are you sure you wouldn't rather stay behind?"

"Quite sure. After all, Brett isn't going to be the only person there. I shall probably enjoy myself in spite of him."

Melanie was silent for a moment, then burst out: "I can't understand his preferring Elaine. He must be out of his mind!"

"She's very beautiful!"

"You're not exactly an ugly duckling yourself, and if you spent as much as she does on clothes you'd knock her into a cocked hat!"

"Evidently Brett doesn't think so."

"Then he's crazy!" Muttering darkly to herself, Melanie bent and kissed Loris and went into her own room to change.

Now that someone shared her secret Loris felt less lonely in her unhappiness and thought ruefully that whoever had said a trouble shared is a trouble halved had certainly been right. The knowledge of Melanie's sympathy made it easier for her to meet Brett on a casual and distant footing, and she no longer disappeared when he called but remained downstairs in the lounge or out in the garden with Dickson.

For his part Brett maintained an impersonal, aloof attitude towards Loris, and did his utmost to conceal his jealousy of Dickson. Sometimes looking down at the boy as he lay in his invalid chair, he wondered whether Dickson had ceased to love Melanie and transferred his affections to Loris. He was aware that

Melanie spent more time with her fiancé now, but could not decide whether it was because she sensed the danger of losing him to her friend or whether it was a genuine desire to be with him, and one afternoon he watched her for some time, unnoticed, as she sat on the lawn with Dickson. The sight of her slim figure made him ache with longing and he knew that if he had hoped to find peace with Elaine, it would never be more than a fleeting oblivion.

Elaine, on the other hand, was more than satisfied with Brett, for he was docile and gentle, and if at times she experienced a faint twinge of conscience, a glance at the large, flawless emerald on her finger served to remind her of all she would stand to lose if she gave him up.

CHAPTER XII

THE evening of the party arrived and there was great excitement as the family got ready, an excitement heightened by the arrival of exotic sprays for the women – a present from Mr. Loftus and Dickson. Melanie was in such high spirits that she ran in and out of Loris's room continually, first for her hair to be approved, then for her nails to be varnished and finally her dress to be fastened; and when at last she was ready, flushed and eager in a white dress spangled with silver stars, Loris felt a catch at her throat at the sight of so much fresh loveliness.

Satisfied that she could not improve on herself, Melanie turned her attention to Loris. "Heavens, you're not nearly ready yet," she chided.

"With you popping in and out all the time I don't see how you could expect me to be," Loris replied with a twinkle.

"Well, now it's my turn to help you. I can't wait to see you in your new dress."

Loris looked dubiously at the black gown lying across the bed. At her last fitting she had been startled to find that what she had envisaged as a simple dinner dress suitable to wear at the vicarage was a sleek, tight-fitting sheath that would have shocked the good people of Roxborough.

But when she had protested, Madame Thérèse had brushed aside her doubts.

"Nonsense, *ma chère*, you look *absolument charmante*. Perhaps it *is* different from anything you've had before, *mais alors*, it's the style you *should* wear. *Ma foi!*" she glanced down at her own bulk, "if I still had a slim figure like yours, I would show it!"

Loris had protested no more, although now, surveying herself in the full-length mirror, she wished she had, for the material clung revealingly to every line of her body.

The dress was strapless, its bodice boned and heavily encrusted with black jet beading which glittered darkly as she moved. It was more sophisticated than anything she had ever seen, let alone worn, and although she had to admit that it flattered her, found herself wishing the skirt did not fit so tightly.

But Melanie thought otherwise and clapped her hands in rapture. "I never knew you had such a lovely figure, Loris – you look gorgeous! Wait till Elaine gets an eyeful of you – she'll be green with jealousy!"

"You don't think it's too tight?" Loris asked anxiously.

"Of course not – that's the style. I wish *I* could wear something like it, but I'm not tall enough – or sophisticated enough – and by the time I am, I shall probably be too fat! Now let me put some more lipstick on you – you haven't enough."

"No, thanks, dear," Loris said hastily. "I'm not a film star, you know."

"Rubbish, you must look your most glamorous at a party. Sit down on the stool and I'll make you up properly. Now don't argue – I'm not going to let you spoil the ship for a ha'porth of tar!"

"Well, just make sure it *is* only a ha'porth," Loris warned.

Melanie ignored the remark. "I'll leave your cheeks pale and put just a touch of eye-shadow and mascara on. Oh, what lovely long lashes you've got!"

Knowing it would be useless to protest Loris submitted meekly to her ministrations, and afterwards peered anxiously into the mirror, relieved to see that Melanie had heeded her warning.

Mrs. Loftus had insisted on lending her a fur jacket, and she carried it on her arm as she followed Melanie out of the room, but half-way down the stairs she remembered her handbag lying on the dressing-table and

116

ran back to fetch it.

The family were waiting in the hall as Loris came downstairs again, moving slowly and carefully on the high heels of her silver sandals, the front of her dress slit on one side, revealing fleeting glimpses of slender, nylon-clad ankles. Her hair was swathed on the top of her head, showing her perfectly shaped ears, the lobes of which sparkled with diamanté ear-rings matching the narrow gleaming criclet round her throat, and as she came towards them each member of the family had a different impression of her.

Dickson from his wheel-chair gave a long, low wolf-whistle which his father, had he been younger and less dignified, would have echoed. Mrs. Loftus regarded her with the complacent satisfaction of a fairy godmother, while Melanie, watching Elaine, felt a thrill of elation at the disconcerted look on the indolent face.

"Isn't she lovely?" Mrs. Loftus murmured. "She didn't want to have that dress made, but I persuaded her."

Secretly disturbed at Loris's undeniable beauty – who would have imagined the self-effacing English girl could ever look like this? – Elaine could cheerfully have consigned her mother to the depths of the Pacific Ocean at that moment. But she grudgingly agreed. "Come along, Loris," she called impatiently, "you're holding us up."

They all moved down the steps and waited while Mr. Loftus and the nurse manoeuvred Dickson into the car, Melanie hovering anxiously in the foreground. At first Melanie had been afraid her presence might embarrass him and that he would prefer her to keep away at times like these, when he was at such a disadvantage, helpless and dependent on others, but now she knew this to have been false reticence on her part and realized that the sooner they treated his paralysis in a normal way the better it would be for both of them.

Within a few minutes they were deposited at the brightly lighted entrance to Brett's large, white house.

Gleaming cars were parked close together in the driveway and the sound of music emanated from somewhere behind the house.

Brett greeted them as they descended the terrace steps and kissed Elaine lightly on the cheek, commending her upon her appearance. He was equally gallant to Melanie and Mrs. Loftus and it was only when he came to Loris that the smile on his face became set. The rest of the family were already moving away and greeting their friends, and for a moment Loris and Brett were on their own.

His eyes travelled over her figure, taking in the lovely contours of her body and lingering for a moment on her white throat and pink lips.

"So you did come to my party after all," he drawled. "I wasn't sure whether you would."

The white dinner jacket he wore accentuated his height and the breadth of his shoulders, emphasizing the deep tan of his face and the blackness of his hair. His firm lips were lifted in a quizzical smile, one eyebrow sardonically raised, and Loris dug her nails into the palms of her hands, refusing to flinch beneath his scrutiny.

"Of course I came, Brett. Nothing would keep me from celebrating – Melanie's birthday and engagement."

She started to move across the lawn and he fell into step beside her. "I hope you won't refuse me the pleasure of a dance later on?"

"Why should I?"

"No reason," he said stiffly. "I just thought you might be too busy with all the other men."

Loris faced him angrily. "I notice that even an occasion like this hasn't sweetened your temper."

"I'm sorry." Brett's mouth twitched. "It wasn't necessary for me to be so unpleasant."

By this time they had crossed the lawn and Loris stopped and looked around for Melanie.

"I expect you'll find most of the guests on the dance floor down by the barn," Brett said, as if reading her thoughts. "I'm afraid I'll have to stay up here until everyone's arrived, so if you'll excuse me –"

"Don't let me detain you," Loris said softly.

With an inclination of his head Brett turned and went back towards the terrace, and Loris made her way through the copse to the clearing, where a large dance floor had been laid down in front of the barn. On a low dais to one side a band was playing, and on the other side groups of people stood around a long bar, talking and laughing as they sipped their first drinks of the evening.

Loris was conscious of interested stares in her direction and was beginning to feel embarrassed by them when a young man detached himself from one of the groups and came up to her.

"My name's Morgan – Dale Morgan," he said, with a friendly smile, "and you're Loris – I know, because Dickson's told me so much about you. Now, what'll you have to drink?"

"I don't really know. To tell you the truth, I hardly ever drink at all."

"In that case I'm afraid I can't get you your usual buttercup of nectar, but I can recommend a champagne cocktail."

Loris hesitated and then nodded. "I'd love one."

"O.K. But don't disappear into the woods, Diana."

He turned away to give the barman his order, and a few moments later rejoined her with two brimming glasses.

He handed her one and held his own aloft. "To Loris the lovely!"

Loris smiled her thanks and sipped. "H'm, delicious!" She took a gulp.

"Hey, go easy! It's got a kick like a mule."

"Tastes like a mixture of lemonade and cider to me."

Dale clapped his hands to his head. "Holy mackerel, you can go on *thinking* that, but just don't drink it as if it was!" He took her by the arm. "Come on over and let me introduce you to the gang."

119

Leading her across to a small group of people standing at the edge of the dance floor he introduced her briefly and informally. They all seemed pleasant and friendly, interested to meet an English girl earning her living in the States, and would have kept her talking about her home and her opinions of their own country if Dale had not propelled her quickly on to the dance floor as the orchestra began to play a tango.

"If I don't dance with you right now I might not get a chance later," he murmured as they moved away together, and he was proved right, for no sooner had they finished their dance than one of his friends approached her and Loris found herself dancing with one man after another, responding lightheartedly to their easy banter and trying not to remember the occasion they were supposed to be celebrating.

Another drink was pushed into her hand and she drank it quickly, conscious of a pleasant headiness, until after an interval during which she seemed to be dancing the whole time, she found herself in Dale Morgan's arms again.

He held her more closely this time and in her unusual state of elation Loris did not find his proximity unpleasant.

"I'm sure glad I found you," he said, putting his cheek against hers, "and I'm not going to let you disappear now we've met. Imagine Dickson being engaged to one lovely girl and keeping another up his sleeve all this time! But I'm going to change all that. How about a date with me tomorrow night?"

"Because I'm a small, untwinkling star?" Loris asked softly.

"Because you're lovely and I've fallen for you in a big way, honey."

Honey! The endearment echoed in her heart and twisted the knife of memory. How long ago it seemed since Brett had held her in his arms and called her that! Hearing someone else use a word she had always associated

120

with him made her realize that although they quarelled bitterly every time they met, the love born of that fleeting nebulous episode on the boat could not be rooted out.

Glancing down, Dale Morgan was surprised at her expression. "Hey, hey, don't look so solemn! You're not scared of me, are you?"

She looked up into the attractive, boyish face. "Of course not." The music stopped and they walked off the floor. "About the – the date, Dale, I'm not sure. Will you ring me tomorrow?"

"I certainly will. What's the best time to –?" He broke off with an exclamation of mock disgust as Brett approached. "Looks as if I'll have to surrender you to our host right now, but don't forget I'll be waiting."

Loris stepped into Brett's arms with a calmness she did not feel and they danced in silence. He held her loosely, an eloquent space between them, until she stumbled a little and his grasp tightened as he drew her closer.

"That's an unusual dress you're wearing, Loris."

"An unusual dress for an unusual girl," she retorted, and then with an archness foreign to her and due to the potent drinks she had had, she added: "It's the first time you've seen me in anything so sophisticated, isn't it? Do you think it suits me?"

"Very much." His lips formed in a half smile, but his eyes were grave.

"I'd have preferred a little more skirt and a lot more top," she went on naïvely, "but Madame Thérèse liked it this way. I gather you don't?"

"Loris, don't talk like a fool." He gave her a little shake. "I believe you're a bit tight."

"I've had several champagne cocktails," she admitted.

"That accounts for it, then. You're not to have any more."

"You've no right to tell me what to do," she said hotly. "I'm not your fiancée, you know."

He did not answer and they finished the dance in silence, coming to rest by the bar.

The sight of it spurred her to an act of defiance.

"I haven't drunk your health yet, have I, Brett? You must at least allow me the pleasure of toasting your engagement."

"You don't want any more to drink," he said curtly, "you've had quite enough already." Never had he seen her in such a mood. She puzzled and excited him as never before, and while part of him wanted to shake her, the other part wanted to gather her close and kiss away the hurt bravado and pain in her eyes.

But she ignored his remark and ordered two champagne cocktails from the bartender.

When they were handed to them, she raised her glass and clinked it against his, marvelling that her hands did not tremble. "Here's to your marriage, Brett. May you have all the happiness you deserve. You have a wonderful home here, and I'm sure Elaine will grace it for you."

She drained her glass, set it down sharply on the bar and then, with an incoherent exclamation, turned and fled.

"Loris, wait –" He moved as if to follow her, but Elaine's voice, cool and amused, stopped him.

"Brett darling, where are you off to?"

He paused and looked down at her, suddenly wondering how, even in the most turbulent state of mind, he could ever have asked her to marry him. As friends they were ideally suited, but as the woman he wanted for his wife, the one person he would have chosen to share his life and be the mother of his children, she, like the rest of her type, fell lamentably short. Not that he did not like her – on the contrary, she amused him with her gaiety and wit. But there was about her the same sophistication and brittleness which he had distrusted in all the other women he had met.

Brett had always told himself he would never marry unless he found the woman of his choice, and he had never been willing to compromise, for the idea of second

122

best was abhorrent to him. In Loris he believed he had found what he had been looking for all his life, and the discovery of her duplicity and deceit had only made his disillusionment the more complete. But now he realized that no matter how much Loris had mocked his ideal of her, no other woman would assuage his need and longing for her, and looking down at Elaine knew he could not go on with this farce of an engagement any longer.

But although he realized that by leaving the engagement even for another day he was only delaying something which would be more unpalatable to her the longer it was put off, he could not bring himself to tell her in the middle of the party being held to celebrate it; at the same time cursing himself for the weakness which had prevented him from telling her before the party had had a chance to take place at all.

"Brett, I've been talking to you and I don't believe you've heard a word I've been saying!" Elaine accused.

He forced his wandering thoughts back to her. "I'm sorry, my dear. What was it?"

"Nothing of any importance," she said lightly, although secretly annoyed at his lack of interest. "Do you know you've only danced with me twice this evening."

"I'm sorry," he said again, "but there were all sorts of duty dances and I –"

"Oh, I know that," she pouted, "but don't let's waste time now. Dance with me, darling."

She slipped into his arms and they began to move around the floor, but Brett danced automatically, his eyes continually straying in search of Loris.

"Brett, you're still miles away," Elaine spoke with some asperity. "What's the matter with you?"

"I was just wondering how Dickson's getting on," he lied. "I've been so busy looking after everyone else that I'm afraid I've left your family to take care of themselves. Do you know where he is?"

"The last I saw of him was in his chair on the terrace. He refused to let anyone wheel him down – said he didn't want to look conspicuous. For all I know he's still there."

"Is Melanie with him?"

Elaine shrugged. "I don't know, and I really don't care. If Dickson's silly enough not to make the most of the little he *can* enjoy, that's his business."

The dance came to an end and they left the floor. "If you don't mind, Elaine, I think I'll go up and see how Dickson's getting on."

She made a little moue of protest. "If you *must* leave me so soon —"

With an apologetic smile Brett moved away and her eyes followed him speculatively across the lawn pondering on the reason for his sudden remoteness.

From a distance the terrace appeared to be deserted. It was faintly lit by the glow of the barbecue fire at the top of the lawn and the air was pervaded by a delicious smell of roasting meat and venison. Brett sniffed it appreciatively and looking at his watch, saw it was nearly time for supper.

He walked up the terrace steps and seeing the wheels of the invalid chair in the far corner, moved towards it, his footsteps resounding faintly on the flagstones.

"Hi, there!" he called. "How're you getting along?"

Dickson, who had been watching the people below him on the lawn, looked up with a start. "'Lo, Brett. You'd never believe how crazy people look at a party! Wonder if I used to behave that way — all that smirking and simpering and idiotic laughter?"

"That's easily answered — you did! Where's Melanie?"

"She was with me until a few minutes ago, but I told her to go and have some fun. It wouldn't be much of a party for her having to sit with me all the time. I guess she's dancing by now. Didn't you see her on the floor?"

"No, but there's quite a crowd, so I probably missed her. It's getting a bit chilly already — I'm glad I had the barn fixed for sitting-out.

"Mind if I draw up a chair and keep you company for a while?" he went on.

"Thanks, but I'm O.K. here alone. I don't expect to monopolize the host."

"Nonsense," Brett said equably. "I've done more than my duty already this evening, and I think I've earned myself a rest." He drew up a chair and sat down. "Cigarette?"

"Thanks." Dickson took one from the proffered case and they smoked together in companionable silence.

Melanie meanwhile was enjoying herself on the dance floor and was whirled from one partner to another until, flushed and breathless, she slipped away to tidy her hair before returning to Dickson. She walked through the copse, humming the tune to which she had just been dancing, but was only half-way through the trees when there were footsteps behind her and she heard her name called. With a start she turned to see Miguel coming towards her.

He caught her by the arm. "Melanie, I have been looking for you all the evening," he said reproachfully. "Can it be that my little darling has been avoiding me?"

She gave a strained laugh. "I didn't even know you were here. Anyway, I've been with Dickson nearly the whole evening – as a matter of fact, I'm on my way back to him now."

"You cannot go back to him yet – I want to talk to you," he said decisively.

Melanie looked uneasy. "I can't stop now, Miguel. What did you want to say?"

He came a step closer. "Never before did you ask me what there was for us to talk about. What has happened between us, my little one? At one time I think you were only happy when you were with me, but now I have not seen you for days and days. When I ring you up you will not speak to me, when I call I am told you are not at home, and when I write to you my letters are never answered." He flung out his arms dramatically. "All I hear is silence, silence, empty silence!"

Melanie glanced anxiously around, for with every passing moment he was becoming more impassioned and eloquent.

"What is it between us, Melanie, my little dove? You are so strange and cold, I cannot understand you any more. I thought we were in love."

Melanie looked at him aghast. "But you know I'm engaged to be married!"

"Pouf, such a silly convention! You love me, Melanie, not your American boy. He is a baby who cannot appreciate you."

"But, Miguel, I *don't* love you." She was growing desperate. "I don't love you and I never said I did."

"There are some things it is not necessary to say," he whispered passionately. "When you let me hold you in my arms and kiss you there was no need for words between us."

"I know I let you take me out," she said, flushing, "but it was only because you were amusing and – and different."

"And you still find me amusing and different, my little one," he said ardently. "You cannot deny it. We are made for each other."

"Don't be ridiculous, Miguel." For the first time Melanie realized how deeply she had involved herself with him and searched for the right words with which to extricate herself. "I'm – I'm surprised you should have taken a few kisses so seriously. I thought someone as – as sophisticated as you would have realized how little they meant."

Miguel opened his lips to protest, but the determined expression on her face showed him that to argue with her in her present frame of mind would be useless. Always before this he had been the one to grow tired, never had anyone tired of him, and his vanity was sorely wounded.

"You cannot let us part without giving me a chance to tell you what is in my heart." Then placatingly: "It is too cold for us to talk here – come into the barn for a little while." He was sure it was only her conscience which made her afraid of admitting her love for him, sure that the moment they were alone together and she was in his arms again he would be able to kiss away her doubts and protestations. "Please, my little one, do not deny me this one thing," he pleaded.

"Oh, very well," Melanie said shortly, "but I hope it won't take long. I must go back to Dickson." Exasperated at the turn of events, she followed him unwillingly back through the copse, afraid that if they stayed near the clearing one or two guests might hear what he was saying. If Miguel was determined to make an exhibition of himself, better if he did so unobserved by anyone else.

When they reached the barn the ground floor was already occupied by several couples, laughing and flirting together, and they made their way up the wooden stairs to the little gallery which ran along one side. Although it was dark up here they could discern a few wicker chairs along the wall, and Melanie sat down on the first one she came to, eager to get the interview over and return to Dickson.

"Well, Miguel, I'm listening," she said severely.

Miguel took her hand, surprised when she drew it quickly away. "But, darling –"

"No, Miguel, it's all over between us. You must understand once and for all that I love Dickson and I'm going to marry him."

"You never reminded me of that when I used to kiss you," he said reproachfully.

Melanie bit her lip. "I admit I was wrong to let you and I'm sorry if it gave you the impression that I – that I was –" she hesitated, finding it difficult to explain.

With an exclamation Miguel knelt at her feet. "I have searched the world for someone as lovely as you. In my own country I never met a girl who would not open her arms to me, but all of them –" he snapped his fingers, his eloquence running away with him, "all of them are as nothing compared to you. Your innocence, your beauty,

127

the magnetism of your elusiveness, have set me on fire, and if you do not return my love you will break my heart."

Melanie's eyes softened. "Oh, Miguel, I'm not worthy to be loved like that! I went out with you and let you make love to me when I had no right to do so. I used you as an escape from boredom – to help me when I was unhappy – without realizing that you'd take it so seriously."

"But Melanie –"

"No, no." She touched his face with a gentle hand. "I blame myself for everything and I can only ask you to forgive me."

"But no, I cannot let you go like this!" he flung his arms wide. "First I must drink to our parting and to your happiness. *Madre de Dios*, I have not even drunk a toast to your birthday! That at least you will not deny me, I beg you. Sit here and wait while I go down and bring up two glasses of champagne. We will drink to the day that brought you into the world, to the sorrow of parting, and to – *mañana*!" And with a flourish he turned on his heel and went down the stairs.

Melanie watched him walk to the door and when he had disappeared sat back with a sigh, lost in thought, unaware of Loris sitting in the shadows at the other end of the gallery.

When she had run away from Brett Loris had been too miserable to go on pretending to a gaiety she did not feel, and had hidden herself away where there was least likelihood of being disturbed. She had seen Melanie and Miguel come up to the gallery and had shrunk farther back into her corner, knowing that if Melanie saw her now she would guess something was amiss, and not wishing to spoil her friend's enjoyment of the party had been an unwilling eavesdropper to their conversation.

She had been surprised at the way the Argentinian had allowed himself to be disposed of and relieved at Melanie's firmness. Now that she had broken with the

Latin it should not take her long to make up her mind about Dickson, and the sooner that was settled the sooner Loris herself would be able to go home with an easy mind. To stay here now would be more unbearable than ever, for she was in no doubt that Elaine would hasten her marriage to Brett and to be there when the wedding took place would be more than she could bear.

She sat huddled in her corner, too dejected to move, until she was roused from her bitter thoughts by a faint smell of burning. Almost immediately there was the sound of a triangle being beaten and a voice from the lawn shouting: "Come and get it!" A burst of talk and laughter greeted the call and she heard everyone making their way up to the barbecue. The dance band stopped playing and the musicians could be heard calling to each other as they moved through the copse to the terrace to play for the guests while they ate.

Loris saw Melanie stir restlessly as though she wished to join the rest of the party without waiting for Miguel, but with a sigh she appeared to change her mind and settled back in her chair.

Suddenly aware that the smell of smoke was becoming stronger, Loris wrinkled her nose in distaste. If this was an American barbecue, then the food must be very over-cooked! She debated whether to go and get some supper, but feeling she could not face a crowd yet, leant back against the wall and closed her eyes.

She did not know how long she had been sitting there before she realized that the smell of burning was even stronger, and was aroused by a faint crackling. With a start she got to her feet and ran to the gallery railing, drawing back with a gasp of horror at what she saw. The floor of the barn was a creeping mass of flame, and tongues of fire were beginning to lick the bottom of the stairs.

She raced to the other end of the gallery, desperately hoping that Melanie had gone, but as she reached the far corner she saw the girl staring with terrified eyes at the

129

wall of fire advancing towards them.

"Oh, Loris, thank God you're here!" Melanie almost fell into her arms. "I was waiting for Miguel and must have been daydreaming. I don't know how a fire could have started so quickly without my noticing it."

"I didn't notice it either. I smelt burning, but thought it was the barbecue."

"I didn't know you were up here at all."

"I've been here quite a long time," Loris said abstractedly, leaning over the gallery railings.

Melanie followed her. "What shall we do? It's impossible to get down the stairs now." She drew back with a gasp as the heat of the flames beat up against her face. "Oh, Loris, I'm so frightened!"

Loris was frightened herself, but realized that if she gave way to her fear Melanie might become hysterical. "We'll just have to try and get down some other way," she said as calmly as she could.

"But we can't! Look, Loris, you can see for yourself – the stairs are going to collapse any moment."

"Then there's nothing for it but to jump. The fire isn't under this part of the gallery yet, so the floor underneath will still be cool."

"But I can't jump, Loris – I can't!" Melanie covered her face with her hands and began to sob.

"You must, Melanie – do you hear me? You must!" Loris shook her. "Here, let me help you off with your dress. Tulle is terribly inflammable and you'll be much safer without it." Feverishly she pulled the dress off, the frail material tearing under her hands. "Come along now, climb over the rail."

As she spoke, Loris tore off her own dress and knotted it to Melanie's so that together they formed a short rope.

"What are you going to do?" Melanie asked tearfully.

"Hold one end of this and when you've climbed over the railings you can hang on to the other end. Then you'll only have about five or six feet to drop when you let go."

"Why don't you tie it to the railings?"

"It won't be long enough if I do – a knot would take up too much of the length. You do as I say." She pushed the unresisting girl over the railings and Melanie clung to the makeshift rope, too terror-stricken to protest.

As Melanie's whole weight fell upon the dresses Loris's arms jerked painfully, wrenching in their sockets as they took the burden.

"Go on, Melanie," she gasped. "Climb down quickly before the material tears."

She braced herself against the swaying weight, and each painful second seemed like an eternity as she strained every nerve to hold on until, suddenly and miraculously, the agonizing pressure ceased and the rope slackened in her grasp.

Leaning over she saw that Melanie had landed on the floor beneath, and watched anxiously as she got to her feet, relieved to see that she appeared all right. Then raising her voice above the roar of the fire she called out to her.

"Run and get help, Melanie. Quickly before it's too late!"

With her hands over her face Melanie ran to the door of the barn and was lost to sight in the clouds of black smoke pouring into the air, and Loris sank back on the floor of the gallery, her eyes smarting and streaming with tears. Everyone was on the lawn and she knew it would take Melanie several minutes to run through the copse. If anyone had noticed the smell of burning they must have imagined it came from the barbecue fire.

She stood up and tried to find a cooler place to stand, for the heat was becoming intense. Unless help came soon it would be too late. The moments seemed like hours and with every second the flames were advancing. Soon they would reach the floor beneath the gallery and then the gallery itself would be ablaze.

She leant as far back against the wall as possible, but even there the heat threatened to overcome her, and after

131

a few moments she realized that her only hope lay in making a bid for safety. Swinging herself over the railing, Loris clung to the bars perilously, looking beneath her to the floor eighteen feet below. Then, shutting her eyes and not giving herself the time to think, she let go and struck the ground so heavily that she was conscious only of a sickening jar before she fainted.

Melanie meanwhile ran through the copse, the night air blissfully cool against her skin after the inferno she had just left. Sobbing for breath, she reached the end of the belt of trees and in the distance saw groups of people seated at the small tables on the lawn. But she was so breathless that her voice was too weak to attract their attention and she ran on towards them.

She had just reached the edge of the lawn when Miguel came running to meet her, two glasses in his hand.

"Sorry I've been so long, but I had to come up to the house to get our champagne." Suddenly he noticed her appearance. "But, Melanie, what's the matter?"

"There's a fire – the barn's on fire!" she gasped. "Loris is trapped – get help, quickly!"

Then, demented with fear, she started to run back the way she had come, leaving Miguel to spread the alarm.

Seated together on the terrace, Brett and Dickson were first aware that something was wrong when they noticed a commotion at the other end of the lawn, but it was too far away for them to see what was the matter and it was only when Miguel rushed up the steps to the house shouting for ladders and a hose that they realized there was a fire.

But even then the seriousness of the situation did not dawn on them.

"What's the matter?" Dickson asked sarcastically. "Is your tablecloth alight?"

"The barn's on fire!" Miguel yelled, "and that English girl's trapped!" He rushed past them into the house. "I'm going to call the fire brigade!"

"That English girl!" The words struck horror into the

two men on the terrace.

"Loris!" With an oath Brett threw back his chair and started to run across the lawn.

"Melanie!" Without stopping to think Dickson pulled the rug off his legs and hardly aware of what he was doing, stood up and started to stumble down the terrace steps.

By the time Brett reached the clearing, clusters of excited people were standing around watching the blaze, powerless to do anything until equipment arrived. Melanie lay on the grass in a state of collapse and one of the men had taken off his dinner jacket and put it beneath her head.

Brett bent over her. "Melanie, where's Loris?"

She looked up with a little moan, and Brett repeated urgently:

"Where's Loris? Where's Loris?"

"She's – she's in the barn – up in the gallery. She told me to run and get help, and then I don't remember –"

Brett got to his feet, staring at the barn in horror. Could anyone still be alive in that inferno? Snatching off his jacket, he wrapped it around his neck and ran towards the fire.

"You can't go in there, Brett," someone called. "It's suicide!"

"There's a girl in there!" he shouted back.

"But for God's sake, man, she hasn't a chance. Don't be a fool!"

Without replying Brett raced on. As he reached the barn door the heat struck him like a living thing and the smoke was so dense that he could scarcely see a yard in front of him. One end of the building was now completely alight and if anyone had been there he knew there was no hope for them. But he remembered Melanie saying that Loris was in the gallery, and looked up at it, seeing with horror that the stairs had collapsed and there was no way to climb up. Despair clutched him as he imagined Loris lying on its floor, quite inaccessible.

probably unconscious from the heat and smoke.

In spite of the jacket shrouding his head, his eyes were beginning to stream and every breath was agony. Knowing it would be useless to call Loris above the roar of the fire, he ran towards the gallery in the hope of finding some way to climb it before the whole building collapsed. But as he passed the burning stairs he stumbled and almost fell over a prostrate figure on the floor, and looking down saw it was Loris.

Such relief flooded through him that for an instant he stood like a man paralysed. Then, snatching off his jacket, he picked up the unconscious girl and covered her head and shoulders with it.

Holding Loris against him so that his body acted as a protection, Brett ran towards the door. Showers of sparks filled the air, singeing his hair and burning his face, and twice he stumbled and almost fell, his eyes blinded with the acrid smoke. Coughing and gasping for breath he passed through the door, and as he staggered out the roof sagged and collapsed with a roar, sending up a sheet of red flame into the dark sky.

Eager hands tried to take Loris from him, but he ignored them all and laid her gently on the grass. Someone had obviously had the presence of mind to call a doctor, for a middle-aged man came forward and bent over her, lifting her eyelids and feeling her pulse. She was so white and still that Brett's heart throbbed with fear lest he had been too late, but after a moment the doctor looked up reassuringly.

"She's suffering from severe shock and multiple burns. We must get her to hospital right away. My car's at the bottom of the clearing, so if you'll help me to carry her to it I'll take her there myself. It'll be quicker than waiting for an ambulance."

Brett lifted the still unconscious girl and followed the doctor to his car. He laid her down gently on the back seat and got in front with the doctor. "I'll come with you, if you don't mind."

The man glanced at him keenly. "Of course not. You look as if you could do with some attention yourself."

"There's nothing the matter with me."

The doctor drove quickly, although to Brett it seemed an eternity before they arrived at the brightly lit entrance to the hospital, and he watched silently as Loris was laid on a stretcher trolley and wheeled away.

A young intern led him into a small surgery off the main corridor, where he proceeded to dress the superficial burns on his hands and face. But Brett was so impatient for news of Loris that he answered the young man's questions about the fire with ill-concealed irritation, and was relieved when he was at last allowed to leave the surgery. Going out into the corridor again he saw Mr. and Mrs. Loftus and Elaine waiting for him, and they moved towards him quickly.

"How is she, Brett? Is she going to be all right?" Mrs. Loftus asked. "When I think of that girl's courage –" She started to cry and her husband put his arm around her shoulders consolingly.

At that moment the doctor reappeared and they turned towards him full of apprehension.

"How is she?" Brett jerked out.

"As comfortable as can be expected. I've given her an injection in case she comes round and her burns are being dressed."

"Is she badly burned?" Mrs. Loftus asked.

"Fortunately she fainted face downwards, but of course she'd taken off her dress and her shoulders and legs were badly scorched. The jump didn't help matters, either. One leg is very bruised and the ankle's so swollen that we'll have to take an X-ray to see if the bone's broken."

"She strained her ankle just a while back," Mr. Loftus put in.

"That accounts for it, then."

"Is she in a public ward?" Brett broke in.

"At the moment she's still in the theatre."

"Then I'd like you to put her in the best room you have."

The doctor nodded. "I'll speak to Matron about it. It's been an unfortunate accident altogether, but I don't think there's any need for immediate anxiety. We must be glad she's no worse. Believe me, I've seen far more terrible results from fire than this. But you won't be able to see her tonight, I'm afraid – I should call up in the morning if I were you. Incidentally, young man," he turned to Brett, "go home as soon as possible, and –" he fumbled in his pocket and brought out a little bottle from which he extracted two tablets, "take these before you go to bed. Now if you'll excuse me I'll go and have a word with Matron."

With a quick, friendly nod he walked away up the corridor and Brett watched his retreating figure until it disappeared. Then he allowed himself to be led out to the waiting car and sat hunched in the front seat as Elaine took the wheel while her parents silently got into the back.

As they drew up outside the Loftus house the older couple stepped out and with a murmured good night went quietly indoors. Elaine backed the car and started off towards Brett's house, but although she glanced at him from time to time she did not speak, realizing that nothing she could do or say would penetrate his absorption.

It was not until they were nearing his home that Brett roused himself sufficiently to ask about Melanie and Dickson.

"Your chauffeur took them both home as soon as you left for the hospital," she explained briefly.

"Was Melanie all right?"

Elaine nodded. "She was as white as a ghost, but I guess it was just shock. Nothing that a good night's rest won't put right."

Brett grunted and slumped back against the seat again, silent for the rest of the drive.

He had no recollection of saying good night to Elaine, and when they reached his house stumbled from the car without a word. Dorcas took him up to his room and gently removed his smoke-grimed clothes and helped him into bed. Then going downstairs, he returned a few minutes later with a cup of hot milk, and watched over his master until he had drunk it and swallowed the pills the doctor had given him.

The old Negro stayed by his side until Brett sank into exhausted sleep, then silently moved across the room and opened the windows. The acrid smell of burning wood still filled the air and in the deserted garden the tables and chairs stood in ghostly confusion on the lawn. The only sign of life was the dying embers of the barbecue fire in the grate below the terrace steps, and a lighted lantern, forgotten and left swinging in one of the trees.

CHAPTER XIII

WHEN Miguel rushed past him into the house and Brett started off towards the barn, Dickson stumbled half-way across the lawn before he was aware of what he was doing. Then the realization that he was walking brought him to a standstill, and in that instant he lost the impetus which had prompted him to move, and fell heavily to the ground.

Cursing, he dragged himself by his hands to the nearest chair, but the muscles which had been disused for so long would not respond and the effort of getting up on it proved too much for him. He sank back on the grass, breathing heavily, and lay there in agony for Melanie, believing it was she who was trapped in the burning barn.

He was aroused by a crowd of people coming over the lawn, one of them carrying a girl, and it was only as they drew near that he saw the streaming golden hair and realized with a sob of relief that Melanie was safe.

Mrs. Loftus suddenly caught sight of her son, half-sitting, half-lying on the grass, his back against a chair, and ran to him with a cry. "Dickson, Dickson, you foolish boy to crawl all this way!"

He brushed her remark aside. "Mother, is Melanie all right?"

"Yes, darling, she's only fainted. But you –" she wrung her hands. "Oh, son, we all forgot and left you on your own!"

At that moment Edward Loftus came up and he and another man carried Dickson up the terrace steps to his invalid chair. The boy was too dazed to do anything but acquiesce, and it did not occur to him to tell his parents he had walked and not crawled across the lawn to the place where they had found him.

Melanie was wan and shaken as they drove home, but

she managed to walk into the house unaided, and waited in the hall while the chauffeur brought Dickson in.

As they arrived the nurse appeared, and Dickson gave her a lopsided grin. "I'm not the patient for you now, nurse. My fiancée's had a pretty bad shock, so she takes precedence."

Clucking sympathetically, the nurse led the unresisting girl upstairs and put her to bed.

Dickson meanwhile wheeled himself through the library into the annexe which since his accident had been converted into his bedroom. His legs beneath the rug felt heavy and alive, and he was conscious of a tingling sensation like pins and needles, as if the blood were coursing through veins unaccustomed to it. He flexed his muscles and as he felt them move the blanket stirred, and beads of perspiration broke out on his forehead.

But he had no time to test them any further, for at that moment the nurse appeared and started to prepare him for the night.

"You've had a shock too, I guess, and the quicker you're in bed and asleep, the better," she said cheerfully as she bustled about.

Dickson submitted to her attentions with good grace, although he refused the sleeping draught she wanted to give him. He could hardly wait to be left alone, and scarcely had she closed the door behind her than he flung off the sheets and swung his legs over the side of the bed.

Grasping the bed-rail, he levered himself up, then with fast-beating heart released his grip and brought his hands down to his sides. Standing on the floor unaided, he moved one slow step, then another, and almost before he knew it had walked across to the window. When he reached it he spread his arms wide in a gesture of release, and leaning his head against the cool glass, sent up a prayer of thankfulness that the use of his legs had been restored to him.

Slowly he retraced his steps, climbed into bed, and lay

139

in the darkness thinking of all it would mean – of the joy it would give him to tell his family, the joy of leading an active life again, and above all of being able to look forward to the future. He would be able to marry Melanie now.

Melanie! Dickson was jerked into wakefulness at the thought of the girl upstairs, asleep and unaware of the experience through which he was passing. Part of him wanted to shout his news from the house-tops, but some restraint, a caution alien to his nature, made him pause to think. He shifted uncomfortably. Should he tell her? Once she knew he was well, there would be no barrier to their marriage. But, strangely, he did not want that. He did not want Melanie to marry him merely because there was no barrier. He wanted to be sure she loved him in spite of any obstacles that might be in the way.

When Loris regained consciousness she did not know where she was, and her eyes roamed the small, white-walled room, taking in its austerity and cleanliness. As she turned her head a spasm of pain shot through her and she found that her hands and arms were encased in thick white bandages.

For a moment she was puzzled, then the events of the fire slowly began to come back.

She remembered clinging to the gallery rail and dropping to the floor below, but after that her mind was a blank and she knew nothing of how she came to be where she was.

As she was beginning to wonder how to attract someone's attention, the door opened and a pleasant-looking nurse came in, her small cap sitting on a mass of dark curls like a cork on high seas.

"Good morning," she said brightly. "So you're awake at last!"

"What time is it?" Loris faltered. "Where am I?"

"It's ten o'clock – a.m. – and this is the Westwood Hospital."

"What time did I get here last night?"

The nurse raised her eyebrows. "Last night! My dear Miss Cameron, you've been here four days."

"Four days? But that's impossible – you must be joking!"

"No, I'm not," the girl said gently. "Your arms and legs were so badly burned that Dr. Marchbanks decided to keep you under morphia to spare you as much pain as possible. But they're healing nicely now, thank goodness."

Loris absorbed this in silence. Then: "How's Melanie?" she asked faintly.

"Would she be the little blonde who's been calling to inquire about you so often? Oh, she's quite all right. You've been inundated with telephone calls and flowers, and my! – you've certainly given yourself some wonderful publicity! Your name's been on the front page of all the newspapers – and your photograph, of course. You're a local celebrity!" Loris gave a faint smile and the nurse went on: "Well, I'll go and get you something to eat – I'm sure you could do with a good breakfast."

Left alone, Loris pondered over what she had been told, wondering who had rescued her and impatient for the nurse to return so that she could ask.

"Here we are!" Balancing a tray on one arm, the nurse pushed open the door. "Orange juice, a boiled egg, some buttered toast and some coffee."

Although propped up by pillows Loris found every movement agony, and was grateful to Dr. Marchbanks for having doped her through the worst of the pain. She was exhausted by the time she had finished the meal, but the nurse seemed pleased with what she had eaten, and stood balancing the tray on one plump hip.

"Now you have a nice little doze again, young lady, and then I'll come in and give you an injection."

She was leaving the room when Loris called her back. "Oh, Nurse, I nearly forgot to ask you – who rescued me?"

"Why of course, you don't know, do you?" the girl exclaimed. "It was someone called Brett Halliday – your host at the party, I guess. Gee, not every girl is lucky enough to be rescued by such a handsome knight-errant!"

So Brett had rescued her – dear Brett had risked his own life to save hers! Weak tears ran down Loris's cheeks, and the nurse looked at her in concern.

"Don't cry, my dear. You're safe and sound and well on the way to recovery. Wipe your eyes and try to get some sleep or I'll get into trouble."

The door swung behind her and Loris lay back, overcome with emotion.

During the following days she was not allowed any visitors, for the doctor was dissatisfied with her general condition. In spite of the fact that her burns were healing, she was still painfully thin and nervous, and although this could be attributed partly to shock, he felt there was more behind it. That there was something between her and the man who had rescued her he did not doubt, for Brett's every gesture and expression as he had waited for news had bespoken a man in love.

For the first couple of days he had haunted the waiting-room of the hospital in the hope of seeing Loris, and seemed abnormally disappointed when he had not been allowed to do so. But three days ago the doctor had been able to give him encouraging news of her condition, and had promised that if things went as he expected, Brett might be allowed to see her before the end of the week.

"That won't do me much good, I'm afraid," the man had replied. "I've been called to New York on urgent business, and I've got to fly out to the East Coast tonight. I expect to be away at least a couple of weeks."

"Well, never mind. By that time Miss Cameron will probably be out of here and then you won't have to bother about hospital regulations before you can see her."

Although Brett smiled politely, the doctor sensed his distress. But the love affairs of his patients were no concern of his, and he shrugged it out of his mind.

Brett was determined not to leave for New York until he had told Elaine he wanted to break their engagement, and after his final visit to the hospital he went straight over to do so.

Parking his car outside the Loftus house, he strode up the steps, not feeling as nonchalant or casual as he looked. As usual, Elaine kept him waiting some time before she appeared, and when at last she came into the room, looking poised and assured in a green trouser suit, he was assailed by a qualm of uneasiness. What if she refused to set him free; if she cared more for her future position as his wife than for his happiness?

But if Elaine sensed his nervousness she gave no sign of it, and helped herself to a cigarette before offering him one. Seating herself on the arm of the couch, she swung one leg gracefully backwards and forwards, puffing competent smoke rings into the air, while Brett moved round the room restlessly.

"Well, Brett?" Elaine's voice was faintly mocking. "You've something to say to me, haven't you? Better get it over. I won't bite, you know."

When he had telephoned and asked to see her alone, she had sensed what was in his mind. Ever since the night of the fire she had realized that not even a feeling of obligation would keep him tied to her much longer; one look at his ravaged face as he had waited in the hospital for news of Loris had told her so much that she had debated ever since whether to be the one to break off the engagement.

Brett came to a standstill and stood looking down into her face, thinking not for the first time how attractive she was. But he was quite unmoved by her beauty, conscious only of a faint feeling of – dislike? Revulsion? But that was ridiculous. She had never done anything to harm him. He was the one to blame for their engagement.

143

"You're right, Elaine. There *is* something I want to say, something that's going to be difficult. But it must be said, for our future happiness depends on it. I know —"

She interrupted him. "You want to break off our engagement, don't you? Isn't that what you're trying to say?"

He stared at her. "How did you know?"

She gave a short laugh. "I'm not blind, my dear. It's been apparent ever since the fire. It was obvious then that you weren't in love with me."

Now she had decided to take the initiative she was conscious of a vicious stab of anger against the girl who was the innocent cause of their engagement coming to an end. But Elaine had always been the sort of woman to face facts. Never one to blind herself to realities, she was clever enough to prefer to give in gracefully rather than fight a losing battle. Better to let Brett think she had also decided their engagement had been a mistake, for she was more anxious at this moment to save her face than to try and keep him.

"Don't look so surprised," she went on. "After all, one doesn't have to be very discerning to realize you don't love me any more. In fact," she shrugged with assumed indifference, "it was foolish of me to take you seriously when you asked me to marry you. Perhaps, like you, I was carried away by the night and the moon and the music. Anyway, it was nice while it lasted." She took off her emerald ring and handed it to him. "Thank you for a lovely engagement, Brett."

Brett looked down at the ring in his hand and then up at her. There was a hard gleam in her eyes and a cool smile played about the corners of her beautifully painted mouth, and for a moment he felt she was laughing at him, as if she were enjoying a joke at his expense.

"Thank you for taking it so well, Elaine," he began awkwardly. "I can only apologize if I've hurt you. I assure you I never meant. . . ."

144

She laughed harshly. "Oh, Brett, don't be so solemn!" Irritation that he should think he could cause her unhappiness made her want to belittle him. It was true he would have been an ideal husband – wealthy, handsome, amusing – but there were other wealthy men, and she was glad that, if their engagement had to end, it had done so without her lies and concealments coming to light.

With a sigh of relief Brett stubbed out his cigarette. "I have to go to New York on business tomorrow, so I won't be here to embarrass you. When I come back I shall do my best to see we don't meet too often."

"You don't have to be so conventional, my dear! Those ideas went out with the Ark. Lots of my friends have broken off their engagements and quite a lot of them still meet their ex-husbands, so why should we be embarrassed?" She gave a wicked smile. "You know, Brett, I'm beginning to think you're old-fashioned!"

"Perhaps I am."

"That's something no one would think of attributing to you, with your reputation as a cynic and breaker of hearts."

He lifted an eyebrow. "I'm afraid I'm overrated. If I used to be a woman-chaser it was only because I was looking for – something I could never find."

"That's what they all say." But although she smiled, a little spark of venom flamed in her. "How will you know when you *do* find the right woman, though? You're very wealthy, Brett. Most girls would marry you for that alone."

"That's a matter of opinion."

"Oh, well," – shrugging – "you'll find out for yourself!"

He looked down at the ring lying in his palm. "I'd like you to keep this as a souvenir of our friendship." Instinctive cupidity conflicted with her pride, and seeing the look of indecision pass across her face, Brett urged: "Please accept it. It's so very much your stone."

"Very well." She took it and put it on her right hand.

145

"Thank you, Brett" – touching him lightly on the cheek. "Now I won't keep you, because you must have a million things to do. Good-bye, my dear."

A fixed smile still on her face, she walked out of the room, and in her bedroom a few minutes later heard his car start up in the drive.

Mrs. Loftus came into the room as Elaine was finishing packing. "Why, Elaine, where are you going?"

"To Washington," Elaine said briefly.

"Washington? Whatever for?"

"To stay with the Forrests. I've hardly seen anything of Douglas's family since he was killed and it'll be gay there just now – the season's just starting and I could do with some amusement. This house has been like a morgue since the fire, Mother, and when Loris gets back it'll be worse, with everyone clucking over her."

Mrs. Loftus was shocked at the venom in her tone. "But what about Brett? What's he got to say about your going?"

"Nothing." Without looking up Elaine continued flinging clothes into her case. "We've broken our engagement."

"Broken your engagement?" Mrs. Loftus echoed.

"Must you repeat me like a parrot, Mother?" Elaine shut the case with a vicious snap. "We've broken our engagement. And if it hadn't been for that pious English girl it might never have happened! She *would* go and focus the limelight on herself at a time like this."

"Elaine, you don't realize what you're saying. You're upset, dear –"

Elaine gave a brittle laugh. "That's what you think. After all I've done, to be baulked at the last moment like this –! But what the hell! They're welcome to each other and they can sort out the mess themselves – if they can. I must fly now, Mother. I managed to get a last-minute cancellation on a plane, so I'll have lunch at the airport."

Too astonished at the news of the broken engagement to take in all she had just heard, Mrs. Loftus followed

146

her daughter downstairs. Elaine drove off with a casual wave of her hand and a "Say good-bye to Dad and the kids for me," and her mother stood looking after her with perplexed eyes. Then with a sigh she turned and went back into the house.

Loris had been in hospital for nearly three weeks before she was allowed any visitors, and the first person to see her was Melanie. There were still thick bandages around Loris's arms and hands, and her hair, which had been badly burned, was dragged away from her face in two unbecoming pigtails, which stuck out on either side and made her look like a rakish schoolgirl. But it was her face which shocked Melanie most, for it had grown so thin that the cheekbones stuck out gauntly beneath the parchment-coloured skin.

Melanie fell on her knees beside the bed. "Oh, darling, it's wonderful to see you again! But how thin you are, Loris – are you sure they're giving you enough to eat?"

"If you saw all the things they tempt me with, you wouldn't ask." Even her voice was different – thin and tremulous – although it still had the same clear tone. "But how are *you*, Melanie? What's been happening since I've been here? It seems ages ago since the night of the party."

"A lot has happened. Elaine isn't –" Melanie broke off and put her hand over her mouth guiltily. "But I promised the doctor not to excite you."

"Now you've got so far, you may as well tell me the rest – otherwise I'll only work myself up into a fever imagining what it might be."

"Bully. I came here all prepared to boss *you* for a change, and here you are telling me what to do already! Well, the great news – *I* think it's great, anyway – is that Brett and Elaine have broken their engagement."

Loris closed her eyes for an instant and was silent, then: "When was that?"

"About ten days ago – the day Brett went off to New York on business. Then Elaine suddenly decided to go

147

and visit her in-laws in Washington. I don't know whether she went to be near him in the hope of patching things up, but knowing Brett I shouldn't think she'd have a chance."

"So there's just you and Dickson in the house now, apart from Mr. and Mrs. Loftus?" Loris asked casually.

"Yes. And the children, of course – Elaine left them behind. Trust *her*."

"Who's looking after them?"

"Mother Loftus is, for the time being, although I think she finds them a bit of a handful. Incidentally, they sent their love and there's a letter from Timothy."

She took a grubby envelope from her bag, opened it and extracted a single sheet of paper covered with a sprawling, childish hand. "*Dere Loris*," she read, "*Im so glad you are beter. We want to com and see you, but the dokter wont let us. Hope you com home soon. Love from Timothy.*"

Beneath this there was a line of indecipherable scribble, with a footnote: "*This is not me. It's from Gillian. She says it means she sends her love, too.*"

Tears rose in Loris's eyes, but she blinked them back. "I'm longing to see the children again."

"And we're longing to have you home. Dickson sent his love, too."

"How have things been between you?" Loris asked.

"Quite good on the whole. I spend most of my time with him and feel I'm beginning to understand him at last. And oh, Loris, I do love him so! I must have been mad to behave as I did at first. I'd give anything if I could wipe it all out and begin again."

"But, darling, it's not important now. You've found out in time, and that's all that matters."

"That's what you think." Melanie's voice was bitter. "You don't know Dickson. It seems as if he can't forget. Just when I feel I'm getting near him he withdraws and becomes unapproachable, and you know he was never like that before. There's obviously something on his mind and whatever it is it's coming between us, although I try to pretend it isn't."

"I'm so sorry, darling," Loris said gently. "But try not to worry about it too much. He was probably very hurt with you and you must give him time to get over it. Being ill has made him more sensitive, that's all."

"I suppose you're right." Melanie glanced at her watch. "Good heavens, I've overstayed my time by ten minutes already! I promised Nurse not to, and here I am bothering you with my troubles into the bargain."

"You're not bothering me, Melanie, I only wish I could help you. It's been wonderful seeing you, and don't forget to come again soon."

Melanie bent and kissed her. "Mr. and Mrs. Loftus want to come tomorrow, and I'll see you the day after, if they'll let me. Bye-bye, darling, and don't think of anything except getting better."

Walking down the corridor, Melanie was so immersed in her thoughts that she almost bumped into an orderly. "Sorry, did I hurt you?"

"Not at all. Anyway, it was my own fault. I can hardly see over the top of these flowers." Indeed, the bouquet the girl was carrying was so large that it was all she could do to balance it.

Melanie looked down into the mass of blooms. "Aren't they lovely!" she exclaimed.

"They certainly are. They're for Loris Cameron, that girl who got burnt in the fire."

"Oh, really?" Melanie asked in surprise. "Who are they from?"

The orderly glanced down at the card. "Someone called Brett Halliday. She gets a bouquet like this from him every day. Gee, it must cost him a packet!"

With a cheerful grin she moved away, and Melanie continued on her way even more thoughtfully.

Mrs. Loftus had taken the children down to the beach for the afternoon, and knowing Dickson was alone, Melanie was eager to get home. Although she could drive, she disliked the thought of sitting at the wheel of the long, low car, and gratefully relaxed as the chauffeur manoeuvred it through the busy streets. Melanie marvelled when she saw girls as young as herself driving enormous coupés, although when she had refused Mr. Loftus's offer to allow her to drive he had merely laughed and said she would soon come begging him to let her take the car out on her own.

She leant back, and as the warm breeze from the window blew through her hair and cooled her hot cheeks she thought of Dickson and the weeks since the fire, wishing with all her heart that those months after her arrival had never been.

Back at home, she went straight out into the garden, and was surprised to find Dickson was not in his usual place on the lawn. "Dickson!" she called. There was no answer, and she walked into the house again. The lounge and dining-room were empty, but when she went into the library she found him lying on the couch, a book in his hands.

"What are you doing in here, darling?" she asked gaily. "Didn't you hear me call?"

"Yes, but I was reading."

"Oh." She was chastened, but sat down beside him, realizing he was in one of his difficult moods – moods which had become so frequent of late that there was scarcely a time when he was his normal self. Briefly she told him of her visit to Loris, and the only time he showed interest was when she mentioned that Brett was sending flowers every day.

"Perhaps something'll come of it after all," he remarked.

"Oh, I hope so. If anyone deserves to be happy, Loris does."

"People don't always get what they deserve. You should know that."

Melanie's lips trembled at his tone, but she changed the subject. "Would you like me to read to you?"

"No, thank you, I can read quite well myself. Why don't you take a magazine and sit down quietly?"

Melanie did as she was told, and for the next few minutes the only sound was the rustling of paper. Dickson glanced at her covertly, tenderness in his eyes. His poor little darling! Why was he tormenting her? Ever since he had discovered he could walk, keeping it a secret had made him irritable and nervous. Purposely he had been showing himself at his worst – made her run errands for him and be at his beck and call, shouted at her and found fault with whatever she did for him, until he had seen her eyes fill with tears and her lips – the lips he longed to kiss – quiver at his harshness.

Suddenly he knew he could not go on any longer in this way – that the position between them would have to be thrashed out once and for all, and that he must be courageous to put her love to the test and find out whether, still imagining him to be an invalid, she would agree to their marriage.

"Melanie, there's something I think we should talk about. Put down your book a minute."

Again she did as she was told, and sat with her hands on her lap, looking so like a little girl expecting a treat that it was all he could do not to walk over and take her in his arms.

"I want to talk about our future."

"Our future?"

"Yes. You came out here to marry a healthy young man, and instead found a cripple. I can't help thinking this must have made some difference to your love for me."

"Oh no, Dickson."

He went on as if she had not spoken. "We're dealing with facts now, Melanie – plain, cold facts. And I think that now, if never before, there should be complete honesty between us. When you first came here, you were very quickly bored. I don't blame you for that – you were young and impressionable and very spoilt, and I was a

151

helpless log." Tears were making Melanie's eyes starry, but Dickson hardened his heart and went on: "Since the fire – in fact, since a few days before, if my memory serves me – you seem to have been making an effort to change. You've spent more time with me and you've stopped going out with my friends – or so-called friends. In fact, one might say you've been acting the part of a dutiful fiancée. All that remains to be seen is whether you'd act well in the rôle of my wife."

Melanie moved across the room and knelt down by his couch.

"I don't blame you for being hurt at my behaviour, Dickson. When I look back on it, I can hardly believe it was me. But I've changed since then – I've changed a lot."

"But have you?" he said earnestly. "That's what I want to know. How can I be sure you won't change back again?"

"There's no way of being sure. You must just take my word for it." She put her arms around him. "You've got to believe me, Dickson. I know you feel you can't trust me, but sometimes there are things one *has* to take on trust, and this is one of them. I've accepted the fact that you may never be able to walk again, and I know that if I want a partner for a dance, someone to ride with or play tennis or golf with, I won't find it in you. But that doesn't matter. I love you, Dickson, and the fact that you can't walk needn't prevent us from being happy together. I'll try to make up to you for what you've lost and perhaps one day I'll be able to convince you that the spoilt child I was when I arrived has disappeared for ever."

Dickson caught her to him in passionate joy. Then, unable to restrain himself any longer, he threw back the rug and stood up.

Melanie gasped and whitened, and if it had not been for his arms around her, she would have fallen.

"Dickson! You can walk!"

152

"Yes, my darling, I can walk."

"But when?" she stammered incredulously. "How –?"

"Since the night of the fire. When I thought you were trapped in the barn, I stood up and started to walk before I realized what I was doing."

"But – but do your parents know?"

"No one knows. When I realized I could walk again, I was suddenly so scared I fell over, and when Mother found me on the lawn she thought I'd crawled there."

"But why didn't you tell her? Why didn't you tell us all?"

"I had to be sure first that you'd marry me whether I could walk or not. I had to be sure that the vows we're going to make for better, for worse, in sickness and in health, really meant something to you, and this was the only way I could find out. Once I could be sure you'd marry me, I was going to tell you the truth."

Melanie drew back as if he had struck her.

"How could you be so cruel? How could you let me – let us all – go on thinking of you as a cripple? Don't you care how much unhappiness you bring the people who love you? Every day I've prayed, prayed with all my heart that God would make you well again. Night after night I've cried myself to sleep. I've watched you lying there and ached with sympathy for you. And all this time, ever since you knew you could walk, you've been playing with me like a cat with a mouse – making me dance like a puppet on the end of a string!" She put up a hand and dashed the tears from her eyes. "I know I haven't behaved very well since I've been here, but it didn't take me very long to grow up, Dickson. Perhaps if you'd had a little more kindness and understanding, it would have taken me even less time. But you were so concerned with yourself and your own feelings that you never thought about mine! *You* had to wait for me to prove whether I loved you enough to marry you as an invalid. *You* had to be sure – one hundred per cent sure – because you had so little faith or courage! You were afraid, Dickson – afraid to find out what I'm really like. I shall never forgive you for your heartlessness to us all – never, never, never!" She ended on a sob and before he could stop her, ran out of the room.

"Melanie!"

Dickson started to run after her, but his legs were still unsteady, and as he reached the door he stumbled, missed his footing and crashed to the floor.

Half-way up the stairs, Melanie halted at the sound of his fall. She turned swiftly and saw him lying on the floor, then without thinking ran down the stairs again and threw herself down by his side, cradling his head in her arms.

"Dickson darling, you've hurt yourself again! Oh, God, I hope you're not badly injured – how could I have said all those things to you? I love you, Dickson, I love you! Of course I'll marry you, I'll marry you whenever you want me to!"

Throwing her arms round his neck, she burst into tears, and he gathered her to him without a word. They clung together, lost to everything except each other, and it was only when they heard Mrs. Loftus and the children coming up the drive that Dickson, with surprising agility, scrambled to his feet, and with Melanie by his side, walked down to meet them.

CHAPTER XIV

TIME passed slowly for Loris while she was in hospital. Reading only held her interest for brief periods, and there were long stretches of the day and night when she lay silent and still in the narrow white bed, her mind going back over those last dreadful minutes before she had lost consciousness in the barn; back further to the misery of her dance with Brett; and further still to the months between their meeting on the boat and the announcement of his engagement to Elaine.

The news that the engagement had been broken occupied her mind almost to the exclusion of everything else. At first she doubted whether Melanie was telling the truth, and wondered if it was just her way of trying to help Loris's recovery. Not that Melanie would deliberately lie, but she was quite capable of embroidering on what she believed to be likely in the hope that giving her wishful thinking the light of day would make it more possible; but when the Loftuses confirmed Melanie's story, Loris was filled with conflicting emotions.

When the first magnificent bouquet had arrived from Brett she had been too ill to know, and by the time she was well enough to take pleasure in the daily gift of flowers he was already thousands of miles away on the other side of America. She debated whether to write and thank him, but as he had not written to her she did not like to be the one to take the initiative, and feared he might think she wished to reopen their relationship because she had heard his engagement had been broken, picturing to herself the faintly cynical smile with which he might receive any letter from her – the look she had seen on his face when he had come upon her reading to Dickson or walking through the house with the children.

She did not try to solve the mystery of his broken

engagement, and wondered whether he had gone to New York to escape from Elaine and also, perhaps, from herself. For she had known by his very glance on the night of the party, from the way his eyes had caressed her, that his desire for her was not dead; that there still existed between them a spark which could be easily kindled into flame, and she wondered whether he feared that by staying in California he might be drawn against his will into a relationship he did not want, and that realizing his weakness, he had probably decided it would be safer to put distance between them.

If all this was merely a figment of her imagination or the outcome of her acute awareness of him, Loris asked herself why he had not written, for nothing could have been more natural than a friendly letter or even a note enclosed with his first flowers. The fact that he had sent neither forced her to the conclusion that his daily bouquet was merely his way of expressing regret that her accident had occurred while she had been a guest at his party.

Brett would have been astonished if he had known what direction Loris's thoughts were taking. His one regret was that he had been unable to see her before leaving California, and he only dismissed the idea of writing because there was so much to be cleared up between them that he felt a letter – or even several letters – would be inadequate. A man who had always regarded letter-writing with distaste, he could not deal on paper with her reasons for ignoring his telephone call from New York, coolness when he had returned from Los Angeles, and most of all with her supposed attempts to steal Dickson from Melanie. Even now he had only to close his eyes to see an image of her in the boy's arms and feel a fierce stab of jealousy at the memory.

No, there were too many things to be explained between them for correspondence to suffice. How could he tell her in a letter that in spite of everything that had happened he still loved her, that in spite of her being in love with another man he wanted her to be his wife?

In the ordinary way he would have ridiculed the idea of marrying a girl in love with someone else, but the depth of his desire for Loris outweighed any objections his logic could find, and he only knew he wanted her – and that the longing to hold her in his arms once more, to watch her and be with her always had become so much a part of him that it never left him for a single waking moment.

He could hardly believe his engagement to Elaine had ended so peaceably, for he had been convinced she would refuse to release him, or at least try to make him change his mind. That she had done neither had surprised him immeasurably, and he was still debating her reasons when he reached New York.

He had to stay there much longer than he had anticipated and though furious at the delay there was nothing he could do about it, for the business deal on which he was engaged was too important to be dismissed. It entailed many long and tedious conferences, and by dinner time each evening he was so tired, mentally and physically, that as soon as he had swallowed his meal he retired to his room and fell asleep almost as soon as his head touched the pillow.

Meanwhile Loris had been told the good news of Dickson's recovery.

"You must hurry up and get well," Melanie said excitedly, "because we've decided not to get married until you can be my bridesmaid."

"But I might be here for weeks yet," Loris protested.

"Oh, no, you won't! I spoke to the doctor today and he said you'll probably be able to come home in about a week."

"Did he really say that?" Loris asked eagerly.

"Yes. And even if he hadn't we'd still wait until you came home. I'll never forget I owe my life to you, Loris." Suddenly Melanie bent and kissed her, drawing away quickly lest she cry.

"Don't make me out another Grace Darling!" Loris said with an unsteady smile. "When I think about my lovely new dress being used as a rope, I don't feel a bit like a heroine!"

"What about mine?" Melanie countered in rueful indignation. "All that material going up in smoke!"

"You're lucky you weren't inside it!" Loris retorted. "Never mind, you'll soon be getting a wedding dress." Then casually: "I suppose Elaine'll be coming back for the wedding."

"I doubt it. She's far too busy enjoying herself in Washington. We had a letter from her the other day, congratulating us and saying her present is on the way, and I suppose that's that."

"How odd! After all, she *is* Dickson's sister, and you'd expect her to be at his wedding."

"Depends on the sister," Melanie said drily. "Anyway, the less I see of her the happier I'll be. I can't stand her at any price!"

Loris smiled at her vehemence. "She's going to be your sister-in-law, darling, so you'd better be careful what you say about her."

"Rubbish! Dickson isn't very fond of her either. But don't worry – I haven't aired my views to Mr. and Mrs. Loftus – they're such darlings, I wouldn't say anything to hurt them." Then, with a lightning change of tone: "Have you heard from Brett?"

Loris flinched involuntarily. "Why should I?"

"No reason – I just thought he might have written. After all, he did risk his life to rescue you."

"I know, and I'll always be grateful. But sometimes I wonder why he bothered."

"Loris, what a terrible thing to say!" Melanie was aghast. "Don't ever let me hear you talk like that again. You're just feeling depressed and miserable because you've been cooped up here so long. When you come home you'll be more cheerful."

"Perhaps you're right. But California isn't home to

me, Melanie. Once you're married there'll be no reason for me to stay. Now all I want is to get back home as quickly as possible and forget everything that's happened?"

"Do you think you'll ever do that?" Melanie asked gently. "Do you think you'll ever be able to go back to living that kind of life? You may not realize it, Loris, but you're not the same person who helped to smooth the parish path or acted as mediator between Mrs. Jones and Mrs. Brown. I'll take a bet that after three months you'll be so bored you won't be able to stand it."

Loris shook her head. "Roxborough's my home and all my roots are there. A few months away can't make me forget all that."

"I didn't say you'd forget it or want to. All I'm saying is that although it was all right for the Loris of the past it isn't going to be all right for the Loris of the future."

"I don't agree – I daren't agree, Melanie. I can't stay here any longer. I've *got* to go back and forget."

Seeing the determination in her face Melanie knew that argument would avail her nothing. "Well, you know best, darling, although I can't see why you're in such a hurry. Oh, I forgot to tell you," she added excitedly. "Dickson and I are going to England for our honeymoon! Won't it be marvellous to see Mummy and Daddy again?"

"Wonderful, darling. Have you written to tell them yet?"

"Yes. I had a reply yesterday. Mummy's absolutely thrilled. It'll help to make up for her disappointment at missing my wedding. But the most important thing is that Daddy's getting better and we shall see them soon anyway. Then perhaps they'll come over here for the christening."

"*First* christening?"

"Lord, yes, we're going to have dozens of children!"

When she had gone Loris lay back smiling affectionately at the girl's high spirits, and thinking how thankful they should all be that things had turned out so well

159

for her and Dickson. His illness had obviously made him more serious and mature, giving him a greater understanding of Melanie which would help him to make their marriage a success.

When the time came Loris was quite sad to leave the hospital knowing she would never see her little room again, or the smiling, fresh-faced nurses in their attractive uniform, and above all that she would no longer see Dr. Marchbanks, to whom she owed so much and whose daily visits she had come to look forward to throughout the long weeks.

The luxurious bedroom awaiting her at the Loftus home was rather overpowering after the simple furnishings to which she had become accustomed, and it was strange not to live to a routine any longer, not to be guided by a clock or a thermometer. It seemed strange, too, not to be in charge of the children, but the Loftuses would not hear of her taking them on again.

"No, my dear," Mabel Loftus said firmly, "you may be well enough to leave hospital, but you still look as though you can do with a good rest. Sunshine and plenty of food are all you have to think about for a long time yet. I can look after my obstreperous grandchildren a while longer, and in any case, you'll soon be busy helping Melanie with her wedding."

Indeed, Loris soon found herself drawn into the excitements of the approaching marriage, and although there were hours at a time when she did not think of Brett, the happiness of the people around her and the pleasure they found in the preparations for the wedding only accentuated her own unfulfilled desire to be loved.

At first planned as a quiet affair, Melanie's marriage now promised to become one of the events of the season, and the little bride-to-be went around in a happy daze. Mr. Loftus had brought the young couple a house as a wedding present – a small, white villa on the outskirts of Bel Air, with a garden and tennis court, and she plunged into the task of furnishing it with joyous abandon.

"I'm glad Mr. Loftus didn't buy us anything grand," she confided to Loris. "I'd much rather we started off like any ordinary couple. It's true Dickson has a good position in his father's firm, but I want to encourage him to take an active part in the business so he'll know that when he does achieve something, it'll be through his own efforts."

Loris was a little surprised at the wisdom of this remark, but the more she talked with Melanie now, the more she came to realize how much her friend had changed. She seemed to have grown up almost overnight, and although she had lost none of her high spirits and effervescent vitality, there were times when Loris surprised a thoughtful look on the young face, a look of consideration and reflection, almost of sagacity. Dickson seemed to have sensed this change too, for there now existed a depth of understanding between the young couple which warmed Loris's heart whenever she saw evidence of it.

Melanie was insistent upon her being chief bridesmaid, although Loris's shyness made her unwilling to be the cynosure of all eyes. She did not relish being pointed out as "the heroine of the fire" and had been relieved that during all the publicity it had caused, she had been in hospital, hidden away fom prying reporters. But she could not find it in her heart to disappoint Melanie, and once more went to Madame Thérèse to have a dress made.

Since she had left the hospital no more flowers had come from Brett and she surmised that he had given the florist orders to stop sending them when she had ceased to be a patient. Mr. and Mrs. Loftus seemed to bear him no ill-will for breaking off his engagement to their daughter, and her absence went so unnoticed that had it not been for Timothy and Gillian, Loris would have found it difficult to believe Elaine had ever shared her parents' home at all. That they heard from her they knew, for more than once Mrs. Loftus expressed annoyance and disappointment at her daughter's refusal to come home for Dickson's wedding, but Loris did not know whether this was merely because Elaine was flouting a family convention or because she hopes that by coming home Elaine might see Brett again and heal the breach between them.

The evening before the wedding Loris helped Melanie to pack for her honeymoon, for Mrs. Loftus had shown herself to be as old-fashioned as any other mother and would not hear of Melanie spending the last night before her marriage in the same house as her fiancé. In spite of all their laughing protests she had insisted on their going to stay with some friends who lived in Beverly Hills, and immediately after dinner Melanie kissed Dickson goodbye and having threatened him with dire consequences if he was late for the ceremony the following day, she and Loris were driven off to spend the rest of the evening with Mr. and Mrs. Gaylord, who were to be their host and hostess for the night.

They were a charming middle-aged couple, who, having no children of their own, were delighted that a young bride was to be married from their house, and Mrs. Gaylord, a small, plump woman with the quick movements of a sparrow, ushered them to their bedroom as soon as they arrived. Furnished in pseudo-English style of which she was obviously very proud, she asked them naïvely whether it was not exactly like a typical English bedroom? Looking at the massive four-poster bed, the large marble-topped washstand which, from a glimpse of the shining up-to-date bathroom, was evidently only for show, Loris restrained a smile and assured her hostess that it was more English than her own bedroom at home.

While they were unpacking their night things and Loris was hanging up the bridal gown and her bridesmaid dress in the heavy mahogany wardrobe, Melanie suddenly mentioned Brett for the first time since Loris had come out of hospital.

"Dickson will be very disappointed if he doesn't come
162

to the wedding. They've known each other for years, you know." Her voice muffled in the folds of the dresses, Loris murmured some non-committal reply, and Melanie went on: "Dickson asked him to be his best man, but this business trip came up, so we'll have to put up with Dale Martin – not that Dale isn't a darling, as you'd probably be able to find out if you wanted to."

Loris turned round. "I?" she said in surprise.

"Yes, you, innocent eyes! You bowled him over the night of the party, and whenever he comes to the house now – and even you must have noticed he's been a suspiciously frequent caller lately – he looks at you with such sheep's eyes that I feel quite sorry for him. You might give him a little encouragement, Loris. After all, he's so eligible – and he's an awfully nice boy, too."

"That's exactly what he is – just a boy," Loris·said ironically, and her thoughts flew to a tall, broad-shouldered man with a firm, determined face, lips that could curve with tenderness and eyes that one minute were gay and laughing and the next steely and cold as ice.

"But he's only a year younger than Dickson," Melanie protested. "That makes him a couple of years your senior, anyway." She sighed. "I suppose you know best, but wouldn't it be wonderful if you got married out here? Think of all the fun we could have! I wouldn't mind being labelled a young matron nearly so much if you were one too!" She chattered on, seeming not to care that she received no answers to her questions and quite oblivious of the anguish she was causing.

Left behind, Dickson felt as if the sixteen hours until the wedding ceremony would drag interminably. But he brightened a little at the thought that some of them at least would be spent in the company of Dale Martin and the other men friends he had invited to share his last evening as a bachelor, and he was wondering restively when they would begin to arrive when the telephone rang and he lunged for it.

"Hallo? Who's that? Why, Brett, you old son of a
163

gun, when did you get back? Just arrived at the airport
– gee, that's great! Sure, I'm fine. Yeah, they're fine, too.
No, Loris isn't here – you've missed her by a minute. She
just went off with Melanie to stop with the Gaylords
overnight – some old-fashioned nonsense of Mom's. I
guess they'll be up half the night gabbing – they will be,
if I know my fiancée! What? No, it might be a bit
awkward if you called her up there. But you'll see her tomorrow. How about coming along to my stag party?
Nonsense, you can't work the night before my wedding!
I won't take No for an answer. You will? Atta boy,
that's grand! I'll expect you right along, then."

Brett put down the telephone in disappointment, for
he had counted on seeing Loris as soon as possible and
was irked at the thought of another night of estrangement before he could talk to her. But realizing that a few
more hours would make no difference and that the girls
would be in a dither of excitement at the Gaylords, he
felt it was up to him to go along to Dickson's party and
see the boy got a good send-off for the morrow.

Dickson himself opened the door to him and they
greeted each other warmly. It was the first time Brett
had seen him on his feet since the accident, and they
thumped each other on the back, both speaking at once,
as they went into the lounge.

"I seem to be the first arrival," Brett remarked, looking round the room.

"All to the good – we can have a pow-wow. It's such
a time since I saw you, and once Dale and the gang get
here there won't be much of a chance of swapping yarns."
He went to the sideboard and poured two whiskies.
"Soda?"

"Please – just a dash." Brett took the drink and raised
his glass. "Here's to you, Dickson. May you have every
happiness."

They sat in armchairs opposite each other and as they
sipped their drinks, Dickson studied Brett, noticing that
he was thinner and looked older.

"I'm glad you got here in time for the wedding, Brett. I'd hate to have had you miss it."

"I'd have come back even if my business hadn't been finished in time."

"But it is, isn't it? Don't tell me you have to go Èast again right after."

"No, thank God. As it was, it took much longer than I thought it would. If I'd had any idea how long I was going to be, I – well, there's something I'd have done before I left."

There was a short silence, but although Dickson sensed the significance behind Brett's remark, he did not ask him it was.

Brett broke the silence by inquring after Mr. and Mrs. Loftus and Melanie, and Dickson responded at some length. But when he had finished, silence fell again, and he became even more sure that there was something on Brett's mind. Normally not a loquacious man, he could nevertheless be an amusing conversationalist, and never before had Dickson found him so remote and preoccupied.

"Have another drink?" he asked cheerfully.

"No, thanks," Brett replied, with an absent smile.

"In that case I'd better wait for the boys – don't want a thick head for tomorrow."

Suddenly Brett wondered how Loris was taking this marriage. He still did not know whether she had been genuinely in love with Dickson or whether his attraction for her had been merely the outcome of the maternal sympathy aroused by his affliction. Did that attraction still exist, now that Dickson was no longer an invalid? At that moment Brett would have given a great deal to know.

With attempted casualness, he asked: "How's Loris?"

"Fine. She came out of hospital about three weeks ago, as thin as a rake and pretty shaky, but she's picked up well, although I think Mom would still like to see her put on some more weight. She's been a colossal help to

165

Melanie. They've been running around from one department store to another like a couple of zanies in a treasure hunt! She's a grand girl, Brett – If it hadn't been for her, I'd never have got through those last weeks before the fire." He paused reflectively, then something in Brett's face prompted him to continue. "You know when Melanie first came out here, a lot of the gang gave her a terrific rush, and like a fool, I encouraged her to go along with them. In fact, if it hadn't been for Loris, I'd certainly have been a back number by now where Melly was concerned. D'you know, I was even contemplating sending her back to England? I might even have done so if Loris hadn't persuaded me not to."

"Loris?"

"Sure." Dickson looked at him keenly. "She was the only one who made me feel I hadn't lost Melanie, and as it turned out she certainly knew her better than I did. Why, if I hadn't taken Loris's advice, we wouldn't be getting married tomorrow! What's more there wouldn't have been any stag party for you to sit at and drink my Bourbon. C'mon now, change your mind and have another!"

Brett handed him his empty glass and Dickson refilled it and his own. When he sat down again, Brett regarded him in silence for a moment.

"I'm rather surprised at what you've just said about Loris, Dickson. You see, I – I've always thought she was rather fond of you."

"Sure she's fond of me – most people are," Dickson grinned. "I'm a nice type, not a sad sack like you." Brett smiled briefly.

"You don't understand. What I mean is, I had the impression she was more than just fond of you. In fact, there was a time when I thought she was trying to rival Melanie."

Dickson stared at him in amazement.

"What made you think that?"

Brett stood up, put his glass on the mantelpiece, and

looked down at the boy. "See here, Dickson, what I'm going to ask you now isn't out of mere curiosity. I don't want to tread on anyone's toes and you know me well enough to realize I wouldn't ask you at all if it wasn't important to me."

"Fire ahead."

"Were you and Loris ever in love with each other?"

"In love?" Dickson echoed incredulously. "Good heavens, you're not serious, are you?"

"More serious than I've ever been in my life," came the quiet reply.

Dickson faced him squarely. "I give you my word Loris and I have never been anything to each other except good friends." There was a pause. "Satisfied?"

"Yes." It was a doubtful answer.

"You don't sound it. There's still something worrying you, isn't there? Get it off your chest, Brett. I'll answer anything you want to ask. Then it'll be my turn to ask how you got the crazy notion Loris ever loved me."

Brett sat down again and leaned forward in his chair. "I came here to see her the day after she strained her ankle rescuing Timothy from the roof of the barn. The house seemed empty when I arrived, so I let myself in and went straight into the lounge." He looked away. "I almost interrupted what I took to be a love scene between you and her."

"A love scene? You must have been dreaming!"

"I wish I had, but it was no dream. Loris was kneeling by your couch with her arms around you and your head on her shoulder."

Dickson thought quickly. Then:

"Good grief, you don't mean you thought that was a love scene!" He started to laugh, but at the expression on Brett's face suddenly realized how much it meant to him, and disregarding his own embarrassment, began to explain what had led up to the scene Brett had misinterpreted.

Brett stared at him incredulously and as the boy fini-

167

shed his explanation such relief flooded into his face that even Dickson was moved by it.

"Gee, Brett," he said, "this must have meant an awful lot to you – I didn't realize –"

"It did. But what you've just said has helped to clear up *some* of the misunderstanding which has come between Loris and me since she came to California." There was a pause. Then: "I fell in love with her on the boat, you see. Now I can go to her and clear up the rest." He stood up.

"Hey, you can't go over tonight, you know," Dickson said quickly.

Brett looked down at his watch. "Of course not," he agreed. "I wasn't thinking. Oh, well, we've waited so long that I suppose another few hours won't make much difference."

He sat down again, his thought plunging into an agony of remorse. How could he have misjudged her so? What a fool he had been not to have believed in her – what a callous boor she must have thought him.

Unable to contain himself any longer, Dickson suddenly burst out: "There's something I want to ask *you*, Brett. No treading on toes or anything like that, but why in the name of all that's holy did you ever get engaged to Elaine? You say you fell in love with Loris on the boat coming over. Then what in the world made you ask my sister to marry you?"

"There was a misunderstanding between us and I was going to try and get things cleared up between Loris and me the night I came over here and found you together." He shrugged. "The rest you know. I met Elaine and she took me along to a party. I got tight and didn't remember anything after that. When I rang her up in the morning to apologize, I found I'd proposed to her."

"You don't *remember* proposing to her?"

"No."

"Then how do you know you did? Oh, don't look so surprised – Elaine may be my sister, but I'm not blind to
168

her faults. When she sets her mind on something, she'll do anything to get her way, and she'd obviously made up her mind to get you."

"You're not –?"

"I certainly am. If you want my opinion, I'd say it's quite likely you never asked Elaine to marry you. Look, Brett, you've been drunk before – at parties and weddings and occasions like that. How have you usually behaved?"

Brett smiled ruefully. "I've always been told I get as close as a clam."

"Ah." There was a note of satisfaction in Dickson's voice. "What did I say? If you ever proposed to Elaine when you were tight, then I'm a Dutchman. She probably made it up, knowing you'd never realize she was lying."

There was a stunned silence. Then Brett said: "Great Scott, if she'd do a thing like that, perhaps there are a lot of other things she –"

But at the moment the door opened and Dale Martin came into the room, followed by several other young men.

Reverting to his role of host, Dickson became light-hearted and gay again and entered cheerfully into the raillery and good-natured teasing which most prospective bridegrooms have to endure. Brett, however, could not enter into the spirit of the party, for there were too many things he wanted to think over, and he excused himself early, saying he was tired after his trip and that unless he went to bed he would not be in fit shape for the wedding.

Truth to tell, he was feeling far from tired. His brain had never been clearer and as he drove home, he went over all he had learned from Dickson, filled with gladness that Loris had never been treacherous and deceitful as he had imagined, and bitterly ashamed that he should ever have believed it of her. His first impression of her loyalty and inherent strength of character had been triumphantly vindicated, and the only flicker of doubt that remained in his mind was why, if she had never been in love with Dickson, she had been so cool to Brett himself on his return from New York.

Back in his own home once more, he wandered through the downstairs rooms, visualizing her at the head of his table in the handsome dining-room or welcoming his guests in the lounge which would make such a fitting background for her loveliness and he was filled with longing for the time when she would grace his house and his life, and he could make up to her for the unhappiness caused by his jealousy and mistrust.

CHAPTER XV

MELANIE'S wedding day dawned bright and clear, and as Loris went in to call her and drew back the curtains the sunlight streamed into the room dappling the apple-green carpet with golden.

Melanie sat up in bed and rubbed her eyes, her fair curls tumbled in disarray, and calmly proceeded to eat her breakfast. Then with a little sigh she slipped back under the covers and Loris took the tray off the bed.

"You don't seem to have lost your appetite – I always thought brides were too nervous to eat!"

"Not if you're marrying the right man," Melanie replied complacently.

"There's probably something in that. But you can't stay in bed – it's nearly nine o'clock already – I'll go and run your bath and give you a call when it's ready. Now, mind you don't go back to sleep again!"

As Melanie bathed, Loris busied herself with her clothes and was laying the silk lingerie on the bed when the girl padded back into the room, her feet leaving damp little marks on the carpet. Flushed from the heat of the water, she looked like a naughty angel, with her hair piled on top of her head and a white terrycloth bathrobe enveloping her small body, and Loris thought how little she had changed since their days at Roxborough together.

Presently Mrs. Loftus bustled in to see how things were progressing, and Loris had never seen her so excited. Normally a placid, controlled woman, her face was flushed and her manner quite agitated as she satisfied herself that everything was going to schedule.

Time sped by and Loris stayed with Melanie until she was almost ready. Then she decided to leave her and go and get dressed herself; but coming in from the bathroom found the girl sitting on the bed, one sheer nylon in her hand and one on her leg, staring into space with such a bemused expression on her face that with a sigh of exasperation, she realized she would have to stay with her, and did so until the shimmering satin gown had fallen into graceful folds about the little figure. She was relieved when Madame Thérèse herself arrived to supervise the bride's dressing and left Melanie in capable hands while she went to put on her own dress.

Surveying herself in the mirror a little while later, Loris's thoughts flew back to the night – a night that seemed so long ago – when she had stood before the mirror in the Loftus house and looked at herself before she went to Brett's engagement party. She sighed – sighed for all the might-have-beens and could-have-beens, had Fate been kinder. Then she shrugged away her unhappy thoughts. This was Melanie's wedding day and nothing should be allowed to spoil it.

Badly singed in the fire, her hair had not yet grown to its original length, but clustered in loose, soft curls around her head, giving her the air of a small boy. Madame Thérèse's idea of a simple bridesmaid's dress would certainly have startled the villagers of Roxborough, for it was off the shoulders, of palest bluish-pink chiffon which clung to her waist and then billowed out like a rosy cloud, swirling about her in folds of misty pinkness as she moved, giving her slimness an appearance of fragility accentuated by her heart-shaped face, still too thin, and the large eyes, shadowed by faint smudges of blue. She put on the large-brimmed picture hat of stiffened organdie of the same colour, and picking up the trailing spray of stephanotis she was to carry, went into Melanie's room.

Even the critical eye of Madame Thérèse was enchanted with her, and she surveyed them both with complacency.

"You are zee loveliest bride and bridesmaid I have zee pleasair to dress since I come to America. *Vous êtes*
172

toutes ravissantes et charmantes, et je m'en fâche d'exprimer mes sentiments!'' She raised her hands, at a loss for words.

The wedding party descended the stairs to find Mr. Gaylord waiting in the hall, resplendent in a black morning coat and grey striped trousers. In the absence of Melanie's parents, he was to give her away, and took her proudly on his arm out to the waiting car.

There were murmurs of admiration at Melanie's radiant loveliness as she walked up the aisle. Walking nervously behind the bride, Loris was embarrassed at the glances she felt upon her, and kept her eyes downcast, conscious merely of a sea of faces around her as they halted in front of the altar and Dickson stepped forward to stand at Melanie's side.

Half-way through the service, Loris moved forward to take the bouquet from her trembling hand, and turning to walk back to her place, her eyes met those of a man in the third pew on the left. For one startled instant she paused, her heart thumping madly, then recollected herself and went back to take up her position.

So Brett had come in time for the wedding after all! She had longed so much to see his dear face again that now he was within touching distance, she was filled with such emotion that her whole body trembled.

As Melanie's voice, clear and sweet, fearlessly repeated her marriage vows, Loris felt tears in her eyes and blinked them away. As the solemn words were uttered in the stillness of the crowded church, and Melanie and Dickson swore to love each other for better, for worse, in sickness and in health, Loris silently echoed the words to herself, feeling in that instant as though she and Brett were the only two people in the world.

'Oh, my darling,' her heart cried out, 'if only it were you and I – in sickness and health; oh, Brett, my love, I would work for you and nurse you – for richer, for poorer, for better, for worse – nothing would matter except that we would love each other and find our great-

173

est riches in that."

But as Dickson placed the ring on Melanie's finger and she turned to kiss him, Loris's dream was shattered and she came back to reality again, nervously clutching the two bouquets and refusing to turn even a little for fear she might encounter Brett's penetrating glance.

When he had seen Loris walk up the aisle, Brett had thought her a thousand times lovelier than he had ever remembered, although, with the perception of a lover, he was instantly aware of her fragility. The soft pink of her gown tinged the whiteness of her skin with a pearly radiance, but beneath the drooping brim of her hat he saw that her eyes were shadowed and there were hollows in her thin cheeks. He realized she was unaware of his presence until she turned to take Melanie's bouquet. Then he saw the startled look leap into her eyes and felt, rather than heard, the sharp intake of her breath. She had immediately avoided his gaze, but he was poignantly aware of her eyes, brilliant with unshed tears, and the tremulousness of her soft, red mouth as she listened to the words of the marriage service touched him as he had never been touched before.

The ceremony over, the bridal procession went into the registry and then wended its way slowly back through the church. Melanie and Dickson were driven off immediately, and Loris, who followed in the next car with Mr. and Mrs. Loftus and the children, laughingly shook the confetti from her dress, and hugged and kissed Timothy and Gillian as a reward for their subdued behaviour during a ceremony which, to them, must have been tedious and long.

Arriving at the house, they made their way into the garden, where a huge marquee had been set up to house the buffet, in the middle of which stood a great fourtiered wedding cake. The guests began to arrive, champagne corks started popping, and Loris found a great many people shaking her hand, congratulating her on her escape from the fire and her rescue of Melanie, for

174

this was the first time most of them had seen her since the accident.

Mrs. Loftus moved among the guests hot and excited, her grey hair slightly dishevelled and the feathers of her hat bobbing against her cheek. "Oh, Loris, I'm so hot – I'd give anything for a cool drink. But I can't stop to get one, with all these people to see to."

"Can I get you something?" Loris asked.

"Oh, would you, my dear? How sweet of you. I'll stay where I am, so you'll know where to find me." And the harassed hostess turned to greet a new arrival as Loris started to make her way towards the bar.

"What can I get you, miss?" the white-coated bartender asked.

Not knowing what Mrs. Loftus would like, Loris ordered the first thing that came into her head. "I'll have a champagne cocktail, please."

"So you're still fond of champagne cocktails?"

With a start she turned round and came face to face with Brett. Their eyes met and Loris's heart began to pound. Had his face always been so tanned and lean, his hair always so vividly dark? How could I have forgotten how tall he is, she thought, how broad his shoulders are! Oh, Brett, my love, you are the only man in the world for me. She half-turned away from him, afraid that he might read the secret in her heart. But to the man watching her she seemed quite calm, her eyes veiled, her face composed.

"The drink isn't for me," she explained, hoping no tremor in her voice would give her away.

"Oh? And who *is* it for, may I ask?" he smiled.

"Mrs. Loftus." She took the proffered glass from the bartender, marvelling that her hands were steady and before they could say any more to each other, a group of people surrounded Brett, thumping him on the back and asking where he had been for so long.

With a little sigh of relief, Loris turned and wended her way back through the crowd to Mrs. Loftus, who took the drink gratefully.

"You'll never know what a boon this is, my dear – I was gasping! By the way, Melanie's been looking for you – I think she's ready to change into her going-away clothes."

"I'll go up to her, then," Loris excused herself and hurried across the lawn, through the empty lounge and up the wide stairs to Melanie's bedroom, pausing on the threshold at the sight of Melanie in Dickson's arms. She made a slight sound as she entered, and still in each other's arms they turned towards the door.

Dickson grinned, quite unabashed. "Have you come to help my wife? My wife. . . ." He repeated the words with lingering satisfaction, looking at Melanie with such adoration that Loris felt a lump come into her throat.

"Break it up, you two," she said gaily. "Melanie'll never be ready in time for you to catch the plane unless you leave her alone, Dickson."

"O.K., O.K., I'll go and change – I feel a bit of a fool in this rig anyway, and it's darned hot, too."

He went out, and Melanie threw her arms around Loris's neck. "Oh, I'm so happy."

They laughed and clung together for a moment, then Loris broke away. "Now come along, darling, let me help you change."

She removed the filmy veil, unhooked the satin gown and slipped it off, and in a matter of moments Melanie was dressed in her going-away clothes, a lemon-coloured shantung suit with white hat, handbag and gloves.

There was a knock on the door, and Dickson poked his head in.

"Ready? Fine! We must make a dash for it if we're going to get that plane."

Although they had hoped to leave unnoticed, crowds of people assembled in the drive and showered them with good wishes and more confetti as they drove off, and Loris stood waving and calling until the car turned the bend in the drive and was out of sight.

Soon afterwards, the guests began to leave and slowly the house and garden took on the deserted, dishevelled air that is the aftermath of any party. Empty glasses were scattered on the tables and plates of half-eaten sandwiches dotted the long buffet table in the marquee. And standing alone on the terrace, Loris wondered if anyone else felt her sudden pang of sadness. Then she straightened herself. 'I'd better watch out,' she thought wryly, 'or I'll begin to get like the spinster aunt who always cries at family weddings!'"

Mr. and Mrs. Loftus were in the hall bidding good-bye to some more people, and Loris wandered across the lawn, idly wondering what had happened to Timothy and Gillian. Her stroll led her to the rose garden, and she sat down on a wooden bench, her hands in her lap, looking around her at the heavy blooms and breathing in their perfume.

It was here that Brett found her, and thought that with her skirts billowing around her like pink petals, she looked far lovelier than any of the beautifully scented roses. His feet made no sound on the grass, and it was only when he was a few feet away from her that Loris became aware of him.

Her breath caught in her throat as she looked up. "Oh – I thought you'd gone."

"Would you have preferred it if I had?" he asked softly.

She did not answer his question and her voice when she spoke was formal and polite. "I haven't seen you since the fire, so I haven't been able to thank you for saving my life." He shrugged, and she went on: "I want to thank you for the flowers, too – they were so beautiful and lavish that they created quite a sensation among the nurses." She laughed lightly. "I expect they miss having them in their rooms now I've left."

"In *their* rooms – did you give them away, then?"

"Oh, I don't mean that," she said hastily. "But you sent so many that it seemed a shame to keep them all for

177

myself, and after I'd had them in my room for a day, I shared them with the nurses." For a moment she wondered whether to make any reference to his broken engagement, but was so sensitive where he was concerned, that she did not wish to invite a snub, and cast about in her mind for something to say. "Did you – did you have a nice time in New York?"

"I did not," he said bluntly. "I was so busy I had no chance to have a nice time."

Remembering the lonely evenings he had spent in his hotel room, dreaming about this girl who was now sitting so calmly before him, more desirable than ever, his tone had a forcefulness of which he was entirely unaware, and Loris recoiled at it.

"I'm sorry, I didn't know. But I'm glad you managed to get back for the wedding." There was a pause, then: "Don't you think Melanie made a lovely bride?"

"Yes. Nearly as lovely as her bridesmaid."

Loris hid her hands in the folds of her dress lest he might notice their trembling. "This *is* a lovely dress, isn't it?" she murmured.

"I wasn't referring to the dress, Loris. I –" He broke off at the sound of voices, and glancing up over the hedge saw Mr. and Mrs. Loftus and their few remaining guests strolling across the lawn towards them. "We can't talk now. May I call for you this evening and take you out to dinner?"

She looked away. "I –"

"Loris, please." He caught her hand so that she was forced to look into his face, and a little thrill of joy ran through her at what she saw there.

"Yes," she whispered, "I'll come."

"Good. I'll pick you up at eight."

He turned on his heel and a moment later she saw him pause and exchange a few words with the group on the lawn before disappearing into the house.

Loris sat on a little while longer in the rose garden, refusing to allow herself to read too much into Brett's invitation. After all, he probably realized she would be lonely now that Melanie had gone, and what could be more natural than out of the kindness of his heart, he should invite her to dine with him that night? But a little voice whispered against this cold reasoning and she felt excited and tremulously happy.

Going to her own room to change for the evening, she looked through her dresses dubiously, wishing she had something new to wear. All the clothes she had bought before Brett's party were now too big for her, and the only suitable one which fitted her was a simple afternoon dress in pale lilac, perfectly plain except for a narrow embroidered belt. But it suited her very well, giving her eyes a violet tinge and making her hair glow more darkly.

When she was ready, she went into the lounge and sat down on the couch, idly turning the pages of one of the glossy magazines piled on a small table in the centre of the room. The clock in the hall was just chiming eight when she heard a car coming up the drive, and a few seconds later Brett appeared in the doorway.

Loris got to her feet and gathered up her handbag and gloves, and watching her Brett wondered whether the hours had dragged for her as they had for him, but her composure told him nothing.

He took her coat and held it out for her. "You'd better put this on. It's getting chilly."

As he helped her into it, both of them were intensely aware of each other, and Brett felt a sudden impulse to put his lips to the nape of her neck where the dark hair curled in tendrils.

They walked through the hall and down the steps to the car. The hood was up against the cool night air, and they did not speak as they got in and drove off in the direction of Hollywood.

Brett was the first to break the silence. "Have you ever been to Don the Beachcomber?"

"No. Who is he?"

Brett chuckled. "It isn't a person, honey, it's a restaurant."

Loris's heart leapt at the endearment and she wondered whether it had slipped out automatically or whether he had been aware of using it.

"Isn't that rather an odd name for a restaurant?"

"Just deceptive. It was started by a man who went over to Hawaii. He thought the food and atmosphere there so perfect that he thought it would be a success here. And it certainly has been – usually it's so crowded that unless one books in advance, one has to wait in a queue."

Loris laughed. "I didn't think there were such things as queues in America. What's it like – the restaurant, I mean?"

"Wait and see."

They were silent again, and Loris leaned back and closed her eyes, tired by the excitement of the day. When she opened them again, Brett was bringing the car to a standstill in a car park and he helped her out and led her over to the dimly lit entrance of the restaurant. There was a small crowd of people waiting outside, and the dark little vestibule was guarded by a swarthy Philippino who allowed them to pass when Brett gave his name.

As the door closed behind them, Loris found herself stepping into darkness, but when her eyes grew accustomed to the gloom, she saw that they were in a large room so faintly lit that she could barely see to the other end of it. The walls and ceiling seemed to be composed of bamboo, latticed like a native hut, and the only illumination came from small hurricane lamps on the tables.

"Let's go up to the bar and have a drink first," Brett said, "you can look around afterwards."

They made their way through the crowded tables to the bar at the far end of the room, and perched themselves on high stools, while a white-coated Philippino bartender stood with pencil and pad ready to take their order.

"You'd better leave the choice to me, Loris. There

aren't any champagne cocktails here!"

Before she could reply, the bartender, his dark eyes bright and eager, put in: "We can get you a champagne cocktail, sir, if the lady wants one."

"Oh, no, thank you," Loris replied hastily, and glancing at Brett in amusement, saw an answering smile in his eyes.

A few moments later two large glasses were placed before them and Loris regarded hers with awe.

She sniffed it uncertainly. "Is it rum?"

"Yes. But don't make a face until you've tasted it. I'll bet my bottom dollar you'll like it."

The glass had a huge, cone-shaped piece of ice jutting out above the rim, and Loris remarked on the size of it.

"I've never seen ice that shape – or size – before. What'll happen when it melts – won't the drink spill over?"

Brett grinned. "You're supposed to have finished it by then, honey." He handed her a plate. "Here, have a lambstick."

"A what?" She looked at the long, flat dish he was offering.

"They're the bones of chops – at least what's left of them when the meat's been taken off. Rather than throw them away they hit on the idea of roasting them and serving them up like this. Take one. Yes, you'll have to use your fingers."

Loris took up one brittle end and bit into it. It crunched between her teeth. "Delicious," she said, and picked up another. And they sat sipping their rum drink and munching contentedly until the waiter came to tell them their table was ready.

"Is it near a wall?" Brett asked the man.

"Yes, sir!" came the sibilant and eager reply.

They followed the little dark-skinned man to the far end of the restaurant, and turning to lay her coat over the back of her chair, Loris saw that their table, although apparently set against the wall, was in fact separated from it by a sheet of plate glass about a foot away from the wall itself. Artificial rain slid down the outside of the glass and looking through the mock downpour, she could dimly discern the outer wall, its bamboo surface twined with large green leaves. The dim lighting, the sound of the rain, and the steady stream of water down the glass, dripping off the leaves of the imitation trees, gave the impression of dining in a jungle.

"This place must be unique," Loris exclaimed, as she sat down.

"It is. And I hope you'll find the dinner I've ordered just as unusual."

"I hope I can see to eat it!"

"I'll take the shade off the lamp, if you like."

"No, I prefer it as it is," she replied hastily, glad of the dimness.

A few moments later the waiter set up a small table next to theirs and started to serve their meal. "I didn't order *hors d'oeuvres*," Brett said. "I hope you didn't want any?"

She shook her head. "American meals are so large anyway that I probably shouldn't have been able to get through it if you had."

"But you ought to eat more, you're too thin."

As he spoke the waiter set down a heaped plate in front of her, placing several bowls of food on the table at the same time.

"What is it?" she asked, looking down at her plate.

"The connoisseur's delight – wild pressed duck, unlike any other pressed duck in the world. They keep the skin on to give the dish more succulence – that's why it's so rich and crisp. Those are Hawaiian pea pods, and that's wild rice. Help yourself."

Loris obeyed, and they began to eat.

"Like it?"

"Love it! It's the most wonderful flavour I've ever tasted."

As they ate Brett pointed out one or two celebrities

dimly discernible in the gloom and they gossiped about them casually. Desert consisted of pineapple flavoured with rum and set alight, and fresh paw-paws, and they finished the meal with black coffee. Loris noticed with a faint tremor that although Brett took out a cigarette, he did not offer her one, and wondered that he had remembered she did not smoke. While he smoked she watched him covertly, studying the firm line of his jaw and the aggressive chin, and wondered why she found it so difficult to keep the conversation going when there was so much she longed to say to him.

"You're not tired, are you?" he asked suddenly.

"Not a bit. What made you ask?"

"Only that you've been looking at your watch."

"Have I?" she said lamely.

He signalled to the waiter for his check. "We've been here long enough."

He helped her on with her coat, and then, with his hand under her elbow, guided her out.

Loris breathed deeply as they walked into the cool air. "I didn't realize how hot it was in there."

They sauntered slowly back to the car, and she settled herself comfortably as Brett backed it out of the parking lot. But they had not been driving for about ten minutes before she suddenly realized she did not know where they were.

"Shouldn't we be near the Loftuses' house by now?" she asked.

"We would be if we were going there," he replied imperturbably, "but we're not. I thought we'd drive down to the shore to have a look at the ocean. I want to talk to you, Loris."

Loris's heart raced, but she did not demur as the car flashed along the wide boulevards until they had left the bright lights of Hollywood behind. They passed large, deserted film studios, dark and silent under the light of the moon, and finally, turning a bend, descended a hill which led them on to the sea road, continuing until they reached a deserted part of the coast and Brett pulled up with the nose of the car nearly touching the sand. He shut off the engine, and they could hear the soft lapping of the waves as they broke with a faint hiss on the beach which looked white and cool in the moonlight.

Brett took out a cigarette and lit it.

"Before I say anything else, I want to apologize for ever having suspected there was anything between you and Dickson," he began abruptly. "My only excuse is that I was so jealous I couldn't think straight."

Loris regarded him with startled eyes. "But – but how did you find out that there wasn't? I mean, you seemed so convinced."

"Dickson told me last night."

"I see." Then: "Why did you ask him?"

"Because the thought that you might still be in love with him was driving me mad."

She digested this in silence, then: "Oh, Brett, how could you ever have thought I was?"

"Before I answer that, my dear, there's something else I want to clear up between us." His voice softened. "Loris, do you ever think of those wonderful days on the boat? Do you ever wish we could turn back the clock and be there again?"

"Why do you ask?" she faltered.

"Because between the time I left you on the quayside in New York and when I saw you again in California, you'd changed so much in your attitude to me that I've told myself over and over again you only looked on it as a shipboard romance." He faced her suddenly. "Loris, why didn't you answer my telephone call from New York?"

"I would have answered it if I'd had one, Brett."

"But I called you up, and you were busy," he said sharply. "I asked Elaine to give you the message and she said she'd ask you to ring me back."

"Elaine never gave me any message," Loris said, thinking quickly.

Brett caught her by the shoulders and looked down into her face. "Do you really mean that?"

"Of course," she said simply. "I never received any message that you'd rung me up. I was very – very surprised that you didn't get in touch with me."

"But I did, honey, I did – that's the whole point. Is that why you were like ice to me when I saw you again?"

She nodded. "Partly. And partly because I was hurt that you'd told Elaine when you were arriving, and hadn't bothered to let me know."

"But I didn't tell Elaine. She found out from Dorcas when my plane was due in, and it was a complete surprise to me to see her at the airport. Did you think –?"

"What else was I to think when you walked in with her, especially after she'd gone out of her way to tell me only too clearly how much you meant to her?"

"How much I – Now look, Loris, let's get this straight. What exactly did Elaine tell you?"

"She said – she said you were the only man she'd – cared about since her husband's death and – and that you felt the same way about her."

"She did, did she?" he said grimly. "Anything else?"

"Only – only that you had a reputation as a lady-killer and that you had just been amusing yourself with me on the boat – that I was too young and unsophisticated ever to interest you for long."

In that instant Brett was filled with a cold, implacable anger against a woman capable of inventing such malicious lies. Throwing his half-smoked cigarette out of the window, he took Loris's hand in his.

"Now you're going to listen to me – you're going to hear *my* side of the story, which is something you should have heard a long time ago. Oh, Loris, why didn't you tell me all this before? Why were you so ready to believe everything Elaine told you?"

"Seeing you walk across the lawn with her arm in yours that day *made* me believe all she'd said, and when you were so cool to me, it seemed to confirm everything.

185

You weren't particularly friendly, you know."

"I know, but you weren't the only one Elaine made mischief with. When she met me at the airport and we drove back home, I was already feeling sore with you for not having answered my telephone call, and then she insinuated –"

"That I was trying to steal Dickson, I suppose?"

"Yes."

"And you believed her!" There was gentle reproach in her voice. "So why blame me for believing what she said about you?"

Brett's grasp tightened. "I shall never forgive myself for it," he said. "But I don't think either of us is to blame for what's happened. You were an unsophisticated girl from a country vicarage," there was tender mockery in his voice, "and I was a cynic, over-cautious and only half-believing that your innocence wasn't merely a pose. If we had been together longer at the beginning, our faith in each other might not have been so easily shaken. But we were still too unsure of each other to withstand her ugly insinuations. If I'd had any idea that Elaine could stoop to such . . ." there was furious vehemence in his tone, "why, I –"

"Then why did you get engaged to her?" The words were forced from Loris for she felt that unless she knew the answer to this, nothing could make her quite believe in him.

Haltingly he told her what had happened that fateful night when he had found her with Dickson – of the party to which Elaine had taken him and of its consequences when he had telephoned her the following morning to apologize for his behaviour. Then he told her of Dickson's belief that he had never actually asked Elaine to marry him and that she had fabricated the whole idea when she realized he did not remember anything about the evening he had spent with her.

"And I guess he's right," Brett finished. "I'm not in the habit of getting drunk, but when I do, I'm not in-

186

clined to do much talking, let alone propose to a girl."

Loris sat in a daze of happiness and relief, finding it hard to realize that all she had hoped and longed for was true – that all the misery was over and there was no more misunderstanding between them.

"Aren't you going to say anything?" Brett asked at last. "Aren't you going to tell me that those days we spent together meant as much to you as they did to me?"

"What did they mean to you?" Loris whispered.

"The end of a long search, the beginning of a dream," his voice was husky. "Oh, my darling, I've loved you ever since."

He drew her to him and held her as if he would never let her go, his lips, tender and warm, resting first against the curve of her cheek and the soft pulse which beat in her throat, then finding her mouth as her nearness enflamed him with desire.

Loris clung to him, her reserve melting as her arms reached up and encircled his neck, her whole being flooded with an ecstasy of desire as her mouth responded to the passion of his own. Forgotten was the anguish and pain of the past months, forgotten the bitterness and humiliations she had suffered, and she only knew that with Brett's arms around her she had reached the haven she had been seeking all her life.

Fearful lest he lose the last vestige of his self-control, Brett drew away from her and Loris rested her head against his shoulder.

"I love you, my darling," she murmured softly. "I love you with all my heart."

"I guessed you did, honey, from the way you kissed me." There was tender amusement in his voice. "I suppose I'd better ask you to marry me now."

She rubbed her cheek against his. "You needn't if you don't want to. We could just have a nice, platonic friendship."

"Like hell we could!" He drew her close again and their lips met in another deep kiss.

Huskily, his mouth hardly leaving hers, he whispered: "It's been so long, honey, and I've been such a fool."

"Let's forget the past, Brett, only think of the future."

His hand caressed her cheek. "How forgiving you are, Loris – believe me. I'll make it up to you." Reluctantly he moved away. "Now I suppose I'd better take you home. But first – when will you marry me? We've wasted so much time already that I'm jealous of every hour we're not together."

Her fingers traced the lines of his eyebrows and came to rest against the firm lips. "I'll marry you whenever you like," she whispered. Then: "But I'd like to be married in Daddy's church – would you mind very much if we waited until we can go to England? Daddy would be heartbroken if he thought I was going to get married without him being there."

"I understand, dearest. I wouldn't want to do anything to mar the happiness of your wedding day – it *is* going to be happiness, Loris, as much happiness as it's in my power to give you."

"Oh, Brett, I'm almost afraid that this joy won't last, and that I'll wake up soon and find it's all been a dream."

"It's no dream. And very soon you'll wake up in my arms and needn't be afraid any more." He buried his face in her hair. "We'll fly back to England, Loris – and if we get there soon, Melanie and Dickson will be able to come to our wedding."

"Is that your only reason for wanting to marry me in such a hurry?" she asked, laughing up at him.

"That's enough of that, young woman – you're learning too fast!"

"Don't you like me sophisticated?"

"I like you just as you are, my heart. Don't ever change." He caught her hand and carried it to her lips, placing a kiss in her palm and curling her fingers around it. Then he slipped off his signet ring and put it on the third finger of her left hand.

"It's much too big for you, honey, but it'll do until

I can get you a proper one."

"I prefer this – it's part of you."

Seeing the starry look in her eyes he pulled her towards him and his mouth pressed down urgently on hers in a kiss that seemed never-ending. Then, reluctantly realizing that it was late and that she had had a tiring day, he put her from him, and they sat for a moment in blissful silence before he leaned forward and switched on the ignition.

The engine roared into life and swiftly he turned the car and they started back along the coast road. Stars twinkled in the dark sky like diamonds on a bed of velvet, and a grey, smoky cloud scuttled away from the face of the moon, lighting the road before them with silver, bright and clear as their future.

Harlequin Presents...

The books that let you escape into the wonderful world of romance! Trips to exotic places...interesting plots...meeting memorable people... the excitement of love.... These are integral parts of Harlequin Presents— the heartwarming novels read by women everywhere.

Many early issues are now available. Choose from this great selection!

Choose from this list of Harlequin Presents editions